# THE RED EARTH

Lexi takes a huge risk going to Kenya to marry a man she hardly knows. It seems only to be expected that her fiancé's family will, initially, be suspicious about her. After all, they are part of the wealthy elite, whereas she is an unknown quantity. However, she's not prepared for the attitude of her arrogant, controlling future brother-in-law. Morgan Tyler seems prepared to stop at nothing to make her feel unwelcome. But Fate plays tricks on them both . . .

JUNE GADSBY

# THE RED EARTH

*Complete and Unabridged*

**LINFORD**
*Leicester*

First published in Great Britain in 2009

First Linford Edition
published 2011

British Library CIP Data

Gadsby, June.
  The red earth. - -
  (Linford romance library)
  1. Fiancees- -Fiction. 2. Fiances- -Kenya- -
  Fiction. 3. Upper class families- -Kenya- -
  Fiction. 4. Love stories. 5. Large type books.
  I. Title II. Series
  823.9′2–dc22

  ISBN 978–1–44480–642–7

Published by
F. A. Thorpe (Publishing)
Anstey, Leicestershire

Set by Words & Graphics Ltd.
Anstey, Leicestershire
Printed and bound in Great Britain by
T. J. International Ltd., Padstow, Cornwall

This book is printed on acid-free paper

# A Leap in the Dark

It had all happened so quickly. Too quickly, Lexi Merrill thought, admitting to herself for the first time that she had perhaps been a little hasty in saying yes to an unexpected proposal of marriage.

But Rusty Tyler was young, handsome, wealthy and exciting, and the proposal had followed a whirlwind romance before Rusty left for his home in Kenya.

There hadn't even been time to buy a ring. He had popped the question on the way to Heathrow. Lexi had nearly driven into the car in front in her surprise.

Marriage was the furthest thing from her mind right then. But she had said yes almost without thinking. How crazy was that!

Since then, they had exchanged infrequent text messages and Rusty had telephoned her, briefly, on her birthday. He had been too full of his recent holiday spent lounging with friends on the beaches of Mombassa to speak of marriage plans, for which Lexi was grateful. Getting engaged was one thing, but marriage needed more time, and a lot more thought.

There really hadn't been much to build a relationship on and already Lexi was experiencing doubts. At twenty-eight, she ought to have more sense, but then, Lexi reasoned, there really was something to be said for *nothing ventured, nothing gained.*

When a ticket for Nairobi arrived out of the blue, she simply went with the flow. And now, here she was in Nairobi's Jomo Kenyatta Airport. Being jet-lagged and travel-weary was probably responsible for those negative feelings that were plaguing her. Once she saw Rusty again, everything would be all right.

★　★　★

Lexi put her suitcase down and looked about her expectantly. The airport was bustling with people, men in flowing white robes, women shrouded in drab black or beautiful in vibrant silks. It made her feel terribly alone and vulnerable in her crumpled cotton suit that had been so impeccable at the start of her journey.

When she heard her name called over the public address system, her heart lurched. She gathered her luggage together and made her way to the Information Desk.

A tall, broad-shouldered man was leaning against the desk. He looked up just as she dropped two of her bags. She felt his eyes scrutinise her from the shade of a wide-brimmed safari hat.

Lexi ignored him and left the bags where they had fallen, since he was not about to rush forward to help her.

'I'm Lexi Merrill,' she announced a trifle breathlessly to the desk clerk. 'I believe you have a message for me?'

'Ah, yes, Miss Merrill.'

The clerk flashed her a courteous smile and indicated the man in the safari suit, who was no longer leaning on the desk, but viewing her with more than a little curiosity. 'This gentleman asked me to page you.'

Lexi blinked at the stranger. The man removed his hat and ran long fingers through an unruly shock of dark auburn hair. She could now see his eyes. They were ice grey and coolly hypnotic.

'*You* are Lexi Merrill?' He sounded astonished.

'Ye-es.' Her acknowledgement was uncertain and she saw his dark eyebrows rise slightly.

'You're not exactly what I was expecting,' his eyes told her, although he said nothing and, nodding his thanks to the clerk, picked up her two heaviest bags.

'Come on.' He indicated the exit with a nod of his head and set off towards it.

'I beg your pardon?' Lexi threw a concerned look in the direction of the desk clerk, but she was already busy with another customer. 'Hey! Just a minute!' she called out to the stranger.

She picked up the rest of her luggage and, pushing apologetically through groups of travellers, hurried to catch up with the tall stranger. He stopped in the doorway and turned to wait for her, impatience showing on his face.

'Put my bags down!' Lexi ordered, her voice coming out in a self-conscious squeak.

'Would you prefer to carry them yourself?'

'Of course not, but . . . ' She looked coolly at the stranger and tried to compose herself. 'I don't know who you are or where you think you're taking me, but . . . '

'Your mother told you never to go off with strange men, eh?'

Was that a hint of a smile?

'I'm sorry,' he apologised, without looking sorry at all. 'I've had a heck of a day and I get the feeling it's not exactly over yet, thanks to you, Miss Merrill.'

'I think some kind of explanation is called for,' Lexi said haughtily, drawing herself up to her full five feet four inches, wishing she was taller, much taller. 'I was expecting to be met by my . . . fiancé.' Why did she have such difficulty saying that word?

The stranger gave a short, derisive laugh and looked away from her, his eyes as cold as steel. He stared for what seemed a long time at the frenetic traffic in the wide road outside the airport. When next he spoke he didn't even bother to look at her.

'Your *fiancé* isn't coming. You'll have to put up with me.' He gave her a long look. 'I'm Morgan Tyler. Rusty's brother.'

'His brother! But . . . I didn't even know Rusty had a brother. He's never mentioned you.'

'No, I guess he wouldn't.'

'Why are you here to meet me and not him? He is all right, isn't he?'

'There's nothing wrong with my brother that a little growing-up won't cure.' Morgan Tyler looked squarely at

Lexi and his expression was one of undisguised dislike. 'Now, Miss Merrill, are you coming or are you going to insist on seeing my birth certificate to prove I am who I claim to be?'

'There's no need for sarcasm, Mr Tyler.' Lexi marched past him, and stepped out into the street. 'Which is your car?'

Now that she had seen his face more clearly, Lexi could see the strong family resemblance, though Morgan Tyler was older than Rusty.

'That's it.' He nodded towards a dusty green safari jeep. The name *Tyler Touring Agency* was emblazoned on the side. 'Sorry about the state of the old girl. I've been on safari and had to drive all night to get here in time to meet you.'

Lexi climbed into the vehicle, aware that Morgan Tyler was watching as she hitched her straight skirt above her knees to enable her to reach the high step of the running board. She was painfully self-conscious of the fact that her ankles and feet were swollen after the long flight and she knew she must look a mess.

'Why didn't Rusty come himself?' she asked, as Morgan climbed into the driver's seat beside her and carefully eased the vehicle out into a noisy, nose-to-tail line of traffic.

The Jeep's gears screeched loudly as he swerved around an island, vying for position with a local bus.

Lexi could feel a dull, sinking feeling in the pit of her stomach as she sensed that all was not as it should be.

★   ★   ★

'Rusty was supposed to meet you and explain,' Morgan said, 'but he chickened out. Typical of my baby brother. He's always been very good at getting himself into one scrape or another, then he just walks away and leaves other people to sort things out for him.'

'What are you trying to tell me, Mr Tyler?'

8

Morgan Tyler looked across at Lexi.

'The engagement is off, Miss Merrill. Rusty isn't going to marry you any more than he was going to marry the other silly young women who thought they'd hit the jackpot. If he'd been any kind of man at all, he would have broken it off before you left England.'

'I see.' Lexi stared straight ahead, shocked into silence.

Why hadn't the news devastated her, reduced her to tears? She should be heartbroken. Instead, she was thinking how strange it was that the sun wasn't shining, that it wasn't unbearably hot and fly-ridden, and that people were busily going about their business quite normally.

There were girls in pretty dresses, young men in smart suits, children playing. There were modern office blocks, broken-down shanty buildings, gaudy advertising boards. Hedgerows spilled brilliant pink, mauve, white and yellow bougainvillaea on to the green verges and dry, rust-coloured earth.

This was Kenya and it was real and she was here and it excited her.

A sudden calm settled over her, superseding the shallow veneer of anger that had touched her at the thought of being let down so badly. Not only let down, but humiliated. Going back home and facing her family and friends was going to be a painful experience, especially since most of them had considered her a fool in the first place. Oh, if only she had had not been so blinded by the heat of the moment!

But now she could be honest with herself. The romance with Rusty had been a mistake from the word go. She didn't love him. He had simply come along at the right time, when she was feeling low and thoroughly disillusioned with life in general. The handsome young man with the auburn hair, sea-green eyes and a knack of turning on the romantic charm, had been the perfect answer to all her problems.

Or so she had believed at the time.

★ ★ ★

They had met at a party, only three months ago. Lexi was fresh from a relationship that had been long overdue to end. Then there was the job. Lexi had been a medical secretary since she had left college. She loved the work, but the stress was beginning to get to her. It was time for a change.

'My life has become too routine,' she had complained to her parents over Sunday lunch one day. 'I'm bored with everything and everybody. I need a change.'

'Oh, nonsense, dear!' her mother exclaimed, as she put another helping of roast beef on her daughter's plate. 'When have you ever been bored? It's just not in your nature.'

'Well perhaps I've changed.'

'Don't be silly, Lexi,' her mother insisted. 'You have lots of interests. Good Heavens, girl, you're never still. Always doing this, doing that.'

'It's not enough any more, Mum.'

'You've got Harry,' Mrs Merrill smiled encouragingly.

'Not any more.' Lexi sighed, thinking of Harry, who liked to slump in front of the tele watching football, clutching a bag of crisps in one hand and a can of beer in the other. It seemed like he no longer saw her. She was simply part of the furniture of his rather staid lifestyle.

'Oh, dear! You've been together now for so long . . . your father and I were just saying the other day that it was time the pair of you got married.'

Lexi sighed again and pushed the food around her plate unenthusiastically. Even her appetite seemed to be half-hearted these days.

'You are still friends, aren't you?' Mrs Merrill persisted. 'Harry is such a nice young man. You know, ordinary, just like us.'

'Yes, Mum,' Lexi said, thinking that *ordinary* was the last kind of man she wanted.

'Perhaps you're a little run down, dear,' Mrs Merrill was suggesting, studying her daughter's face closely. 'You do work far too hard, you know. And I've noticed how pale and listless you've been lately.'

'I'm fine, Mum, really I am.'

'I don't think you look after yourself properly,' her mother went on. 'Do you eat enough when you're in that flat of yours?'

'I eat very well!'

'Salads! How can a body function on nothing but salads?'

'Oh, let's not start that again, Mum.'

Mrs Merrill was of the opinion that a person wasn't well fed unless they had at least one hot meal every day. Salad was something one provided for Sunday tea with ham and tongue and a supply of cakes and tarts — traditional north of England fare.

'I still don't understand why you had to move out to go and live in one of those awful flats. I mean, what's the point? You have all the home comforts here with us.'

'Now, now, Enid!' Lexi's father

13

waved his fork at his wife. 'Leave the lass alone.'

'She's still our daughter, Reg.' Enid Merill's voice became tremulous and tears threatened to flow.

'You're over-reacting, as usual, love,' her husband said, as he reached over and patted her hand.

Enid Merrill got up from the table and hurried into the kitchen where she clattered the dishes defiantly.

'Take no notice, lass,' Reg Merrill said. 'You're headstrong, just like me. And like me, you'll make mistakes. But you'll learn from them. Life's a game of chance, Lexi. If you don't gamble with it occasionally you might as well dig yourself a hole in the ground and lie down in it.'

Lexi got up and kissed her father's cheek.

'Thanks Dad. You're quite a philosopher on the quiet, aren't you?'

He patted her hand. 'Aye, lass. It comes with age and experience.'

And it was that evening that Lexi met

Rusty Tyler at her cousin's birthday party.

★   ★   ★

'Lexi, I'd like you to meet the son of an old school chum of mine.' Philip, her cousin, had propelled her across the room and halted her in front of a disarmingly handsome young man.

'Rusty Tyler, meet Lexi Merrill, my cousin and a very nice girl into the bargain.'

And so a new episode in the life of Lexi Merrill had begun. Rusty could not have been more charming. By the end of the evening he and Lexi had laughed, danced, shared a plateful of hors d'oeuvres, and started a mutual admiration society. Their fate, it might have been said, was sealed.

'Where did you get your fabulous tan?' Lexi asked Rusty.

'Oh, I'm just here on a flying visit.' He put another glass of wine in her hand and she accepted it regardless of the fact that she felt she was already beginning to float. 'I live in Kenya. Just outside Nairobi, to be exact.'

'How marvellous! I've always been fascinated by Kenya. What's it like? Is the earth really red like they say it is? Can you actually see wild animals roaming free? Oh, it seems such an exciting, romantic part of the world.'

'Not half as exciting or as romantic as this corner of the world tonight,' Rusty said, staring so intently into Lexi's eyes that she felt herself blush. This is ridiculous, she told herself. He's at least five years younger than I am.

'You're devastatingly attractive, Lexi.'

He was stroking her long, light brown hair and his touch gave her a shiver of delight.

'Look, Lexi, I don't have much time, so you'll have to forgive me if I seem to be rushing you. I think it's highly possible that I'm falling in love with you. Can I see you again? Tomorrow . . . and the next day . . . and the day after that? In fact, I don't want to be separated from you for a moment.'

'Well . . . I . . . ' Was she really hearing this?

'You can feel it too, can't you . . . the electricity . . . ?'

Lexi nodded wordlessly.

'See you will see me again, won't you?' A pair of sea-green eyes searched her face.

'Yes . . . yes, I think I'd like that.'

'What time can I pick you up tomorrow morning then?'

'Hey, I'm a working girl, remember! I'll be free tomorrow evening. You can pick me up at eight.'

'In that case . . . ' He grinned and pulled her to her feet.

'Where are we going?' she asked, as he led her out of the room and down the dimly-lit hall.

'I'm looking for a nice private corner,' he told her, a catch in his voice. 'If I don't get to kiss you soon, Lexi Merrill, I think I'll go mad.'

She had laughed with delight, not

sure what to make of this distinctly gorgeous young man who was like no-one she had ever met. The tiny, warning voice at the back of her mind faded and died. She was ripe for being swept off her feet, and Rusty Tyler had all the qualifications required for the job.

★   ★   ★

The week that followed had been a contrast to Lexi's normal routine. She took time off from her job and showed Rusty the local beauty spots. In the evenings he wined and dined her. At no time did he try to take advantage of the situation, for which she was both glad and maybe a little disappointed. But, she kept reminding herself, they had only known each other a matter of days. It would hardly be wise to plunge headlong into a relationship at this early stage, even if Rusty did look like some bronzed god from a far and distant land.

Then, all too soon, Rusty was winging his way back to Kenya and things settled once more into the old routine. Sometimes it seemed hard to believe they were engaged. Still, Lexi worked her required notice at the hospital and put her flat up for sale. Then the airline tickets arrived. They were attached to a sumptuous bouquet of red roses. Lexi sat holding them in her hands, while her emotions swung like a pendulum.

Suddenly, the dream she had been living for the past three months had become reality. She really was giving up her life in England to go out to Kenya and marry . . . well, a stranger.

She ought to have known that things were bound to go wrong.

Rusty hadn't even met her at the airport. Here she was, instead, with his brother, a brother she hadn't even known existed, and he was telling her that Rusty had changed his mind. The engagement was off. And all she could feel was relief.

* * *

'Here we are.' Morgan Tyler stopped the Jeep in front of a long, low building set back in a side road away from the bustling Nairobi street. He jumped out, not bothering to help her, and handed her luggage to the two African porters who came forward.

'Where are we?' Lexi asked, staring dazedly at the patterned red brick boundary walls, the high trellis with its leafy green foliage disguising what was beyond. Above the trellis there was a hint of mock Tudor walls and a steeply sloping pagoda roof. This, surely, was not Rusty's home.

'It's the Norfolk Hotel.' Morgan acknowledged the respectful salute of a uniformed doorman. 'I've booked you in here for a couple of days. They know to charge everything to my account. You'll find tickets for your return flight to England in your room.'

'I see.' Lexi didn't like Morgan Tyler's officious tone. After all, it wasn't her fault that things had turned out the way they had. 'It seems I've caused quite a lot of trouble for you, Mr Tyler,' she said.

'You're not the first. No doubt you'll not be the last.'

'What's that supposed to mean?'

'My brother is young and naïve, Miss Merrill. He is also wealthy. The resultant combination makes him easy prey to women like you, who think all their problems will be solved by becoming a member of the Tyler family.'

Lexi stared at Morgan open-mouthed. She wanted to defend herself but somehow the words refused to form in her brain. Maybe that's because he was half-right, she told herself ashamedly. She had, indeed, thought that Rusty was the answer to her problems, but not quite in the way his brother meant. Money had not entered into it.

Well, this time she really had messed things up hadn't she? Still, it didn't give this man the right to condemn her out of hand so readily. It was, after all, his brother she'd mistakenly got involved with, not him. Heaven help any woman, she thought, who gets involved with *this* member of the Tyler family!

'Your plane leaves for England tomorrow morning,' Morgan Tyler called from the Jeep as he started up the engine. 'Make sure you don't miss it. There's a possibility of a strike. I'd hate to see you stranded here.'

Then he was gone in a puff of blue exhaust smoke and a squeal of hot tyres. Lexi was left staring after him, rubbing at the sudden spread of gooseflesh that had risen on her forearms.

# A Change of Plan

Fresh out of the shower and wrapped in a complimentary soft towelling bath-robe, Lexi lay on the bed in her hotel room and stared about her, wondering what to do next. The Tylers hadn't exactly penny-pinched when they had booked her into The Norfolk. Her 'room' had turned out to be a luxurious mini-suite with a balcony overlooking an attractive courtyard where there were huge acacia trees and two aviaries full of brightly coloured tropical birds. Also displayed in natural surroundings were remnants of bygone pioneer days — an original covered wagon, a canopied horse-trap and an old iron tractor.

The hotel had been famous for many years. There was a long line of famous visitors, including Winston Churchill, Teddy Roosevelt and Ernest Heming-way.

An atmosphere of historic, yet comfortable opulence, pervaded every corner. It nestled in the centre of Nairobi like a vitally throbbing heart, memories of the past mingling with the present day like friendly ghosts at an eternal house party.

The barely intrusive 'burring' of the telephone brought Lexi reluctantly from her reverie. She wondered who could be phoning her. Only the Tylers knew she was here.

Lexi picked up the receiver. 'Hello?'

There was a long silence, then an uncertain catch of breath followed by Rusty's unmistakable voice.

'Lexi?'

'Oh, it's you.' She couldn't help the sharpness in her voice and hoped he'd noticed it.

Another silence, then: 'Lexi, I'm sorry, really I am! I've behaved atrociously, but I just didn't know how to handle the situation.'

'So you sent your big brother to do your dirty work.'

Lexi swung her feet to the floor. She wanted to sound hurt, just to pay him back, but somehow she couldn't quite pull it off.

'I know I should have come to meet you . . . faced you myself. But the thing is . . . well, Morgan thought . . . '

'Do you always do what your brother tells you, Rusty?'

'Lexi, I'm sorry. I know it makes me look bad, but . . . '

'Rusty . . . please! Let's not go there, eh?'

'But you must be feeling pretty rotten, out here all alone in a strange country.'

'Well, there's not a lot I can do about that, is there?'

'Morgan says he's booked you on the next flight back to England. I suppose there's nothing for it but for you to head back home. I'm so sorry.'

'I'll survive.'

'Lexi, I'm so sorry!'

'I do wish you'd stop saying that. It doesn't exactly help, you know. Anyway,

I don't know if I want to go straight back home. This is a long way to come for nothing.'

'What do you mean?'

Lexi took a deep breath. She had come to a decision.

'I've always wanted to see Kenya, ever since I was a little girl. And here I am. I couldn't possibly go home without seeing something of the place.'

'You mean, you're staying, after all that's happened?'

'Why not? Of course, I'll have to find a smaller, cheaper hotel. I couldn't possibly afford to stay on here. Maybe you could recommend somewhere?

'Oh, but . . . '

'Don't worry, Rusty! I have no intention of being a burden to you. In fact, I'm almost grateful to you for getting me out here.'

'I . . . er . . . yes, sure . . . of course, Lexi, but . . . '

'Rusty, you weren't the only one to make a mistake. My mistake was thinking I was in love when I was in a very vulnerable state of mind. What I'm trying to say is, don't feel too badly about all this. If you hadn't backed out, I would have sooner or later.' She heard a click as if the receiver had been put down, but she knew by the slightly laboured breathing at the other end of the line that Rusty was still there listening to her. 'Rusty?'

'Yes . . . all right, Lexi. It's just, well, it's a bit of a blow hearing you say that. I mean . . . well, I thought . . . '

'You thought I'd be devastated and you're disappointed to find that I'm not.' Lexi, feeling that she had the upper hand, pressed on. 'I'm actually relieved, but I doubt if your brother would believe that. He thinks I'm some fluffy-headed little gold-digger who only wants you for your money.'

'Morgan's like that, I'm afraid. He doesn't have much faith in women.'

'I take it he's not married, then?'

'He's been divorced for years.'

'Really?' Why was she not surprised? 'He got married when he was younger than I am now, to one of those fluffy-headed little gold-diggers you've just mentioned,' Rusty told her. 'The romance was as short as ours and the marriage didn't last more than a couple of months. She ran off with some old American millionaire who promised her more than she could ever have being married to a Tyler.'

'Poor Morgan!'

'You could say that. On the other hand, you could say it was a lucky escape. It wouldn't have been a happy marriage. Mind you, Morgan would never admit to that. And he never talks about that episode in his life.'

Lexi was beginning to relax now that the tension between herself and Rusty had eased. 'Look, Rusty, I really would like to stay in Nairobi for a few days, but not here in The Norfolk.'

'What's wrong with it?'

'Nothing's wrong with it. It's fabulous! It's just way beyond my budget.'

'Let me get back to you, okay?'

'Yes, but don't leave it too long. A

week in this place will cost an arm and a leg! And I'm out of a job, remember!'

'Oh, no! I forgot about that. Oh, I'm sorry . . . '

'If you say that word again, I'll scream. Look, what's done is done. And maybe it was meant to be. Or not meant to be.'

'You really are a nice person, Lexi. Far too good for me. I'll get back to you about the hotel. I promise.'

★ ★ ★

An hour later, Lexi, dressed in a fresh mint green shirt and cool white cotton trousers, made her way down to the hotel foyer. The doorman flashed her a smile. Touching his cap with a white-gloved hand, he gave a bow and asked if he could call her a taxi.

'Thank you, but . . . no . . . I . . . ' Lexi looked around her, squinting in the blinding light of the afternoon sun. 'I'm just looking for somewhere to have lunch.'

'Lunch, madam? Please ... our Verandah Restaurant is very good ... very cool ... many English people, see ...'

The doorman pointed to the left of the doorway and there, indeed, was a very cool looking verandah set out with white clothed tables. Well, Lexi thought, Morgan Tyler had told her to put everything on his bill, so why not.

The menu was surprisingly cheap. Lexi ordered an avocado stuffed with prawns and chicken and a side salad.

It was strangely surreal sitting there, sipping chilled white wine and watching the world go by. And the world here was a far different place than the world Lexi had left behind in England. Outside, on the wide street, there was a bustle of colourful activity.

Silk-suited businessmen jostled with holidaymakers decked out in safari gear and strung with cameras; bare-footed African youths sold yesterday's newspapers and last month's magazines from the roadside to drivers, while younger boys set themselves up on every corner with shoe-shining kits.

A sudden crescendo of English voices attracted Lexi's attention and she turned her head to see what was causing the noise. A small group of homeward-bound tourists, who she had passed in the hotel foyer earlier, had come out and were milling around a tall, confident figure who looked vaguely familiar. It was Morgan Tyler.

He had changed his clothes and shaved off the overnight stubble. He smiled down at the women in the party and they did all but worship at his feet. Lexi found herself staring hypnotically at him, yet dreading the moment when he would look up and see her sitting there, only a few feet away.

When he did finally look her way, regarding her with raised eyebrows and a fading smile, she felt her heart sink down to the pit of her stomach, where it remained, fluttering and fearful. This uncontrolled, physical reaction at the sight of Morgan Tyler took her quite by surprise.

Morgan excused himself from the group of fawning females and walked over to Lexi's table. He stood over her, a solid, muscular figure in khaki. She could see the women looking after him, their eyes jealously flickering over the young woman who had attracted his attention away from them.

'Have you had a good lunch?' The corners of his mouth lifted slightly into an obligatory smile, but his eyes remained as cold as ice.

'Yes, thank you,' Lexi replied politely, her face set and unsmiling.

'The Norfolk has an excellent reputation for the quality of its food.'

'Yes, it is good.' She wished he wouldn't stare at her like that.

'I've arranged for you to keep your room for a week.' He was leaning forward now, both hands placed on the table. 'I take it that will be long enough? Of course, if the air strike goes ahead, you may find yourself faced with a longer stay.'

'I . . . I don't understand . . . '

'Well, you do want to stay on in Kenya for a while longer, don't you?'

'Did Rusty tell you that?'

'Let's just say that I heard it on the grapevine.' His mouth twisted into a lop-sided smile and she felt a sharp spasm of anger grip her.

'So it was you listening in to my conversation with Rusty! I thought there must be somebody else on the line. I didn't expect you to lower yourself that far.'

He frowned, then straightened up and shoved his hands into his pockets.

'Regardless of what you think,' he said tightly, 'the room is yours for a week. Take it or leave it. Personally, I'd rather you followed my original suggestion and flew back to England tomorrow. The sooner we all get back to normal the better. Your prolonged presence here can only lead to complications.'

'Don't worry, Mr Tyler!' Lexi snapped back at him, and then

lowered her voice as one or two heads turned in their direction. 'I have no intention of bothering you or your family any further. My relationship with your brother is over. My only regret is that he didn't have the guts to tell me before I gave up my job and flew out here. However, since I am here it would be foolish not to take advantage of the situation. That way, the whole venture hasn't been entirely wasted.'

'That's exactly why I've booked you in for a few days longer.' His eyes sliced through her like white-hot ice. 'It's a decision I made against my better judgment. Something tells me that you are trouble . . . '

'I beg your pardon! How can you possibly say that? You don't even know the first thing about me.' Lexi said angrily.

'It's a gut feeling. I got it the minute I laid eyes on you.'

'In that case, I suggest you stay well away from me.' Lexi stood up abruptly, knocking her chair over. She flushed scarlet and made a hasty apology to the waiter who rushed to her rescue.

'I have every intention of doing just that.' Morgan Tyler gave a humourless smile and picked up her bill from the table.

'Give me that!' Lexi made a grab for the bill, but he whisked it away and thrust it into the waiter's hand, together with a fistful of notes.

'I can pay my own way, you know. I'm not exactly destitute!' Lexi said.

'But you soon will be, thanks to my brother's stupidity and your obstinacy.'

He reached out and held her arm in a grip that sent a strange weakness straight to her knees. 'I'm sorry you've got yourself into this situation and I'm trying to help. At least do me the courtesy of accepting it with good grace. As for your hotel room, they're not charging me for it. The manager owes me a few favours.'

'Please let go of me!'

She pulled away from him and stood

feeling humiliated and breathless.

Morgan shook his head and gave a deep sigh. 'Just remember to stay away from Rusty. He's too vulnerable at the moment to know what he's doing, especially when it comes to attractive young women.'

So he considered her to be attractive. Well, that was something, anyway, but did he have to make it sound in some way insulting?

'Rusty isn't the only one who's vulnerable,' she said.

She swallowed back the lump that had arisen in her throat and brushed past him, her head held as high as she could get it. She wasn't about to let Morgan Tyler see that her emotions were getting the better of her.

★　★　★

She stormed out of the hotel and turned left into the street, without having the slightest notion where she was headed. She just knew she needed to put as much distance between her and Morgan Tyler as possible.

And yet, if he hadn't taken it upon himself to meet her, she might have been stranded at the airport and at a loss as to what to do next.

Why couldn't Rusty have told her that he didn't really want her? Why couldn't she have swallowed her pride and broken off the engagement herself, instead of allowing things to get this far? Lexi considered herself to be as big a fool as Rusty. Bigger.

Whichever way you looked at it, Morgan Tyler must think her a brainless idiot. And he would be right, too.

A blast on a car horn made her pull up smartly and jump back on to the kerb. She stood there feeling foolish. Some black youths in colourful clothing leaned out of the passing car and grinned at her, waving and shouting.

Taking a deep breath, Lexi picked her way more carefully through the teeming traffic. The sun beat down on her bare head and scorched her fair skin;

the heat from the pavement burned through the thin soles of her sandals as she walked.

The heat was beginning to get to her and she searched hopefully for a place that might offer some shade. The tiny cafés and bars in this part of town didn't look too inviting. Perhaps the best thing would be to go back to the hotel where she knew she could sit in cool comfort and order freshly squeezed orange juice.

Just as she was about to turn back, Lexi spotted what appeared to be an indoor bazaar. People were coming and going, tourists mainly, clutching oddly-shaped souvenirs wrapped in brown paper and string. She could see beyond the entrance and it looked cool and shady and not too crowded.

Well, she thought, I did want to see the local colour. Besides, I may want to buy some souvenirs, so I might as well see what they have to offer.

Boldly, she crossed the road, dodging in and out of the traffic, and stepped inside the market place. It was certainly cooler in here, although the air was musty and thick with the scent of wood and warm spices.

Tiny open fronted stalls were crammed with goods, mainly wood and stone carvings, wicker furniture and raffia bags and baskets to suit every taste.

'You buy something from me, lady?'

A young man appeared at her side, smiling brightly. Lexi soon found herself being steered expertly to his stall.

'There, see! Best in all Nairobi. You buy from me. I sell you what you want: Good price! No better price in all Kenya.'

'Yes . . . thank you . . . everything is lovely, but . . . ' Lexi shook her head apologetically. 'I have no money.' She had left the hotel in such a hurry, she had forgotten to change her traveller's cheques.

'No money, lady? Ah, no! You American, you have money . . . much money. You buy from me.'

'I'm not American, I'm English, and I really don't have any money today. Today I'm just looking, not buying.'

'Ah, English! Okay, okay, lady. You look. You choose what you want. I make special price just for you. Pay tomorrow.'

Lexi was beginning to feel claustrophobic as more young men gathered around her, plucking at her arms to attract her attention to their stalls, which were all very similar.

Lexi kept smiling graciously at them while trying to move on, but they wouldn't let her go. Her way was barred on all sides. She felt a tight feeling in her chest as panic set in.

'I'm sorry, I . . . ' she backed away. She looked at the first young man. 'Please would you tell them that I'm very sorry, but I really do not have any money with me.'

There was a babble of Swahili as all the young men talked at once.

Lexi felt a shakiness creep all over her and she began to sway. Please don't let me faint! she prayed.

The first young man had turned away and was addressing someone who had no difficulty pushing his way through the pressing throng of eager vendors.

Despite the flow of fluent Swahili, Lexi recognised Morgan Tyler's rich tones and relief flooded through her.

She could see the dark auburn head above the crowd, then that stern, bronzed face with its glacial gaze, as he pushed through to her.

'Well, are you coming, or are you planning to spend the rest of the afternoon here?' he said.

Morgan Tyler held out a hand to her and Lexi walked towards him on legs that still felt like jelly. As she reached his side, he placed a supporting hand beneath her elbow and she found herself leaning against him thankfully as they walked out into the bright sunshine.

'I'm beginning to wonder if you're safe wandering about on your own,' he said, and for the first time his smile seemed genuine and lit up his face, although it faded immediately.

'You needn't worry about me, Mr Tyler,' Lexi said, painfully aware of the telltale shake in her voice. 'Normally, I can take care of myself. It was all just a bit unexpected back there.'

Morgan shrugged his broad shoulders and propelled her on, his hand still very firmly holding her elbow.

* * *

At the Norfolk Hotel, Lexi was glad to sink down in one of the comfortable lounge chairs and sip the chilled sparkling white wine that Morgan had ordered for her. He bade her a brief farewell and she thanked him for all he had done. This, she thought, was the last time she was likely to see either of the Tyler brothers. Unaccountably, there was a dull, heavy feeling dragging her spirits down at this realisation.

'There's a problem!'

She looked up, startled. Morgan was

back, staring down at her.

'I'm sorry?'

'The strike. The air controllers have come out earlier than expected.'

'I don't understand. I wasn't planning to leave tomorrow anyway, remember?'

'They need your room. The people who were planning to leave today are still here . . . or will be when they get back from the airport.'

'But where will I go? I'm stranded too, remember.' Lexi was aghast; how could he stand there and tell her she had to give up her room, having just told her she could stay for a week?

'It's all taken care of. Just go and pack your things. You can stay at Redlands until the strike's over and you can get a flight back to England.'

'Redlands? But . . . but isn't that . . . where you live?' Lexi stared up at him, open-mouthed.

'Yes . . . and before you start arguing about it, there's no real choice. Every hotel that's worth staying in is full, thanks to the strike. Besides, I figure we do owe you something after all.'

'That was a quick change of heart.'

'It's not just a woman's prerogative, you know.' He smiled again and something inside her melted.

# Lexi Meets Morgan's Family

The Tyler Estate was on the outskirts of Nairobi, on the road to the Amboseli National Park. Redlands was a collection of white walled, red pantile-roofed buildings nestling in 150 acres of cultivated land.

Lexi couldn't help exclaiming with delight as Morgan drove through the stone pillars at the entrance to the estate with its arch of purple cascading bougainvillaea, followed by a long avenue of tall, yellow-barked acacia trees.

'How lovely!' she enthused, momentarily forgetting her indignation at being ordered about like so much unwanted baggage. 'I had no idea it would be like this!'

'What did you expect? A mud hut out

in the bush?' Morgan looked over at her and the corners of his mouth twitched into a mocking smile.

'Of course not,' she snapped back at him. 'I just thought . . . well, I don't know what I thought . . . Rusty didn't say much about it . . . Goodness, I've never seen trees like these before!'

'They're fever trees,' Morgan slowed the Jeep to a crawl so she could admire the scenery; she was embarrassingly aware of his cool eyes watching her. 'It's actually a type of acacia, but a long time ago a group of people on safari camped beneath these trees and ended up with a nasty bout of malaria, for which they blamed the trees.'

'Malaria!'

'Of course, it wasn't the trees that caused the malaria, but the mosquitoes. This type of acacia grows near water. There's a stream over there, although it's dried up at the moment. Malaria-carrying mosquitoes are usually found near water, hence the name, fever tree.'

'I see. Oh, good grief!' Lexi had

spotted a group of black-skinned natives standing a few yards off. She paled when she saw the long spears the men carried, the immense height of them, the elongated, open ear lobes weighted down with ornaments. There were one or two young women in the group with beautiful faces, shaven heads, perfect teeth and beaded bodies.

Morgan stopped the Jeep and the group approached curiously.

'Masai,' he explained. 'They're good people.'

Lexi swallowed hard and tried to look unconcerned, but she had to control a strong desire to edge closer to Morgan as the tallest of the young warriors came up to the vehicle. His smooth ebony skin glistened in the strong sunlight. His hair, Lexi noticed in fascination, was tightly plaited in long thin rope strands and caked with the red Kenyan earth.

The young Masai warrior spoke to Morgan, but it was Lexi his eyes were fixed on.

A quick exchange of Swahili followed between the two men. Lexi listened, fascinated, until she became aware that they were discussing her for part of the time and her cheeks grew uncomfortably hot, so she made a clumsy pretence of searching for something in her bag.

The young Masai stepped back finally, clasping to his chest a brown paper parcel that Morgan had handed to him. His eyes were full of gratitude.

Morgan restarted the Jeep and they moved forward. Lexi peered through the rear window at the Masai standing in the red dust cloud the Jeep's tyres had stirred up. Hands and spears were raised reverently, then they moved slowly off, long legs striding effortlessly across the parched earth.

★　★　★

'You speak their language very well.' Lexi looked across at Morgan Tyler's chiselled profile; it was an interesting

48

face, strong and full of character . . . and there was a hint of something else. Something deep and private, perhaps born of a hurt and bitterness that he kept locked behind a stony façade.

'Just about everyone in Kenya speaks some Swahili,' he replied as he concentrated on the winding road ahead, which was little more than a dirt track. 'It's the second national language.'

'You seemed to know that young man very well. What was it you gave him? From the look on his face it might have been the crown jewels.'

He shot her a quick glance, and then went back to staring ahead. 'To Mbatian it was probably worth much more than the crown jewels. His wife is sick. I brought him medicine from Nairobi.'

'Oh, I see. So that's what all the talk was about.'

Morgan grinned. And just for an instant, he looked ten years younger and Lexi could see that he must have looked pretty much like Rusty at some time, although the firm mouth and powerful jaw line set him apart from his younger brother.

'Actually, no,' he said. 'We talked mainly about you.'

'Me? What on earth were the pair of you saying?'

Morgan laughed again and hesitated slightly, as if deciding whether or not to reveal the conversation he had shared with the Masai.

'He wanted to know if you were my woman,' he said finally.

Lexi fell silent and stared down at her hands, which suddenly felt like lead in her lap. His woman, indeed! What a thought!

'I trust you put him right on that score!' she managed to say.

There was a short laugh from Morgan. 'I tried!'

'What does that mean?'

'Mbatian considers himself to be something of a prophet. He says the spirits sent you as a gift for me. He says that you were created especially for me.'

'What nonsense!'

'You don't have to believe him.'

'That's a relief, because it sounds like a lot of rubbish to me,' Lexi said derisively, but when Morgan turned and looked at her with those ice grey eyes, her heart tripped and stumbled.

'I've never known Mbatian to be wrong,' he said, then he smiled, and she knew he was teasing her. 'Don't look so worried, Lexi. In less than a week you'll be safely back home in England and all this will fade like a bad dream.'

'Can I quote you on that?' she said and turned her head away, but not before she had registered, with an unaccountable lurch of her heart, that he had called her Lexi for the first time.

★　★　★

'Well, here we are,' Morgan said, and the sight that met Lexi's eyes caused her to sit up and gasp in delight. 'Welcome to the Redlands homestead.'

'This is your home?' She couldn't

51

keep the astonishment out of her voice as her eyes swept over the rambling, white-walled Spanish hacienda-style building with its many archways and low sloping roofs. There was more bougainvillaea, yellow mimosa trees and a profusion of huge hibiscus blooms. The air was heavy with an intoxicating fragrance that lifted the spirit.

'Shall we go in?' Morgan was lifting her bags out of the back of the Jeep.

'Morgan! Morgan!'

They both spun round at the sound of a girl's voice and watched as a horse and rider approached at full gallop. The horse, a jet black stallion with a long flying mane, skidded to a halt in a shower of dust and a scattering of gravel. Its rider leapt agilely to the ground and threw herself bodily at Morgan, who had no option but to enclose her in his arms as they staggered and almost fell.

'Christine! Good grief girl, steady on!' Morgan regained his balance and pushed the girl away, holding her at arm's length. 'I didn't know you were back home. Why aren't you at university?'

'Oh, that!' She pulled a face. 'Who needs it? I've dropped out. Daddy put up a bit of a fuss at first, but I talked him round.'

She was young, Lexi noticed. Probably no more than nineteen or twenty. She was also very beautiful, and knew it, judging by the way those dark eyes gazed up into Morgan's face. The full, pouting mouth however, had just a hint of discontent at the down-turned corners.

'Aren't you going to introduce me, Morgan?' The girl turned an unfriendly gaze towards Lexi.

'This is Lexi Merrill.' Morgan made the brief introduction. 'She's going to be staying with us for a while.'

'Oh?' Christine pulled off the silk scarf she was wearing and shook out her long, nut-brown hair, which fell luxuriantly to her shoulders.

'Hadn't you better see to that horse

of yours?' Morgan looked over to where the stallion was trotting purposefully away. 'We don't want to have to send out a search party again.'

'The boys will see to him,' Christine told him dismissively and slid her arms about Morgan's waist, all the time her eyes on Lexi, half mocking, half curious. 'Aren't you pleased to see me?' she wheedled.

'Right now, Christine,' Morgan extricated himself from her embrace and his voice held a touch of annoyance, 'I don't have much time. I have a business meeting in half an hour and a multitude of telephone calls to make before dinner. Why don't you go round to the stables and find Bobbie? She'll be pleased to see you.'

'I didn't come here to see Bobbie.' Christine spoke softly and the look she gave Morgan needed no explanation.

Lexi looked away, feeling uncomfortable. The girl was obviously in love with the owner of the Tyler Touring Agency. Whether he recognised this fact, was impossible to tell. His face remained passive; his smile only slightly warm, and those incredible eyes betrayed nothing.

'Go on, Christine, see to Ebony, there's a good girl. I didn't give him to you so you could neglect him. Off you go . . . now!'

The girl's eyes flashed angrily and flickered once more over Lexi before she flounced away, beating her riding crop against her high leather boot.

Morgan's cool gaze followed her as she walked away from them. Then he turned abruptly and walked past Lexi without a glance.

'Come on, you might as well meet Belle.' The words were thrown casually over his shoulder.

'Belle?' Lexi asked as she followed him down a long, cool, dimly-lit passage, its white walls adorned with brightly-coloured Masai blankets and a variety of African objets d'arts.

'My stepmother.'

There were other passages and doors

leading off the main hallway, but Morgan continued straight on through the house to what, Lexi assumed, must be the back. The door facing them at the end was half open. As they approached, a woman's strong voice could be heard arguing on the phone. 'I'm not going to be fobbed off with feeble excuses. That feed your company delivered last week was no good. It was already rotting. Now, that's just not good enough, Charlie, so I shouldn't argue if I were you . . . Right! Twenty-four hours and not a minute more.

'Bye, Charlie.'

While she was talking, Belle Tyler had smiled broadly at Morgan and Lexi and beckoned them to come in. She replaced the receiver and swept off her spectacles before getting up to greet them.

'Morgan, darling! I didn't expect to see you for another fortnight! What brings you home so unexpectedly? And who is this?'

Belle Tyler was a large, handsome woman. Her skin was bronzed from long hours spent under the African sun. Her eyes were warm and friendly and her mouth seemed to be permanently fixed in a genial smile.

Lexi liked Morgan's stepmother the moment she laid eyes on her.

Morgan put an arm about his stepmother's shoulders and kissed her cheek affectionately. 'Change of plans all round, I'm afraid. Can you stand a house-guest for a few days? Because of the blasted strike, Lexi here is stuck like a lot of other folk who expected to leave, but can't. And there are no hotel rooms left.'

Still smiling, Belle said, 'Ah, so you are Lexi!'

'Yes,' Lexi said with a rueful smile. 'I'm afraid I am.'

'No matter. I heard it was over before it began.' Belle shot a glance at Morgan. 'These young men! Always causing trouble for themselves and others because they don't know their own minds! It's a great pity it couldn't have been settled before you left England. I gather you gave up your job, too! That's a bit hard. But never mind. You're welcome to stay with us. I think the least we can do is make you feel at home while you're here. Organise some drinks, will you, Morgan? You can pour me a triple whisky. It's been a heck of a day and I need to relax. Lexi, come on to the veranda and tell me all about yourself.'

★ ★ ★

Belle Tyler led the way through to a shady veranda and they sank on to a cushioned sun hammock and swayed gently as they talked. Belle got her glass of whisky which Morgan brought himself, and a few minutes later, a beautiful black girl in a loose fitting white cotton dress brought out a tray laden with tea and fruit cake.

Morgan indicated the tray. 'I thought you might appreciate a cup of tea right now.'

'Yes . . . thank you,' Lexi said, taking the cup he handed her.

'Where's Rusty, Ma?' Morgan asked.

'Oh, Morgan! Don't call me that ridiculous name! He went out riding with Bobbie. Goodness, I don't know what's wrong with that child these days . . . ' Belle leaned over and patted Lexi's arm. 'Bobbie is my foster-daughter. My husband died soon after we took her in, so Morgan, here, is practically the only father the girl has known. She was left on our doorstep, would you believe! She was only a few hours old.

'We never did find out who her parents were. I'd guess that one was Masai and the other was white, but who is anybody's guess.'

Lexi looked across at Morgan and couldn't help noticing the shadow of worry that crossed his face.

'Morgan, you're very quiet. What's wrong?' Belle asked.

'Just a bit tired, that's all, Belle.'

Morgan replaced his cup and saucer

on the tray and stood up. 'If you'll excuse me, I have things to do before dinner.'

'Go! I want a chance to talk to Lexi, anyway . . . girl-talk.' Belle blew him a kiss, which he returned with a smile and left without a further word.

Lexi watched the older woman refill her glass, topping it up with dry ginger this time.

'I'm really very grateful to you, Mrs Tyler,' she said.

'What on earth for? And please call me Belle. Look, my dear, when Rusty came back from England and told us he was getting married, I must admit I was greatly relieved. He and I have never hit it off. He's not made in the same mould as his brother. I'm probably not being very fair to him, but well, he was very young when his mother died. When I came in and took over, he seemed to blame me for everything, including Martha's death. His father died soon after, so you can understand how it must have hit him.

'Morgan, on the other hand . . . well, he and I have always got along. We were firm friends long before I ever married his father, which was more than I could say for Morgan and his mother. There, now, I shouldn't speak ill of the dead, but oh, she was a flimsy, weak-willed creature! Thank goodness Morgan takes after his father. But what am I doing bending your ear with family secrets when I haven't known you five minutes. Morgan would give me a lecture if he found out.'

'Don't worry, Belle. I don't think you need worry. Morgan doesn't like me enough to have much of a conversation with me.'

'You sound disappointed.'

Belle looked over the rim of her glass, her eyes questioning, her smile sympathetic. 'You don't have to answer that, my dear. I haven't met a female yet who doesn't fall in love with Morgan thirty seconds after meeting him. The trouble is, he's embittered by his first marriage, which was an atrocious failure and

61

should never have happened. Still, that's all in the past and it's time he got over it. What's your story, Lexi?'

Lexi lay back against the cushions and watched the great burnt orange African sun slide down behind the clouds. 'I met Rusty at a party,' she began and the story began to unfold.

★   ★   ★

'So!' Belle contemplated the empty glass she now held in her hand, then her questioning eyes sought out Lexi's. 'Now that you're here, how do you really feel?'

'I was fed up with the way my life was going back home.' Lexi spoke firmly. 'I was on the rebound from a relationship that had gone stale. Just when I was feeling the need for something magical in my life, along came Rusty. I suppose he was feeling desperate about something too, now that I come to think about it.

'Anyway, we both got carried away by

some kind of freak, but opportune, slip-tide. Obviously, I can't speak for Rusty, but for myself there was a short, wonderful time when I really did believe that I was falling in love with him. But once he boarded his plane back to Kenya, it all seemed like some crazy, impossible dream. Had I been totally honest with myself, I would have come to the conclusion that I wasn't really in love with Rusty. Not in the way a woman loves the man she hopes to spend the rest of her life with.'

'I'm glad. That would have made things more difficult . . . for all of us.'

'I'm sorry?' Lexi looked puzzled.

Belle smiled. 'Nothing! Just a thought that you might not appreciate at this moment in time. Do go on, my dear.'

'Well,' Lexi continued, 'when my plane tickets arrived, almost out of the blue, I didn't stop to think. I needed something different in my life and here it was being offered to me on a platter. It was a selfish, foolhardy gamble, I admit that now, but I've always had a strong craving to visit Kenya, ever since I was a little girl. I think that's what pushed me, I'm ashamed to say.'

'Which is why you insisted on staying, rather than hopping on the next available flight back to England?' Belle smiled. 'I can understand that. I'd do the same thing myself. So the least we can do for you while you are here is to make sure you do see Kenya, or at least a small part of it. Rusty's behaviour was deplorable. It always is, I'm afraid. He's constantly trying to show his brother and me how big and manly and independent he is. However, I doubt he'll ever catch up with Morgan.'

'You're very fond of Morgan, aren't you?' Lexi asked the question timidly, feeling that she was prying into affairs which did not concern her, yet she was gripped with a driving desire to know more about him.

'I love him only slightly less than I loved his father.' Belle got up and crossed to the drinks cabinet. 'There could be no greater love than the love I had for my husband. I only hope and pray that one day Morgan will find such a love for himself. He deserves it. His first marriage was a disaster. Unfortunately, it seems to have taught him too harsh a lesson. One day, please let it be soon, he'll meet somebody who'll make him forget the pain. It's a great pity, Lexi, that you are not staying in Kenya.'

Lexi caught the implication in Belle Tyler's words. The thought sent a quiver through her.

'Oh no! Look at the time!' Belle was squinting at her watch. 'Come on, Lexi, I'll show you to your room. You'll just have time to shower and change for dinner. The Bensons are dining with us this evening. They're old family friends. We're meeting for drinks on the patio at seven. Wear something cool and casual.'

# A Disturbing Encounter

Lexi was feeling decidedly nervous as she made her way downstairs that evening towards the distant babble of voices already well into social conversation. In the long main hall she hesitated, wondering which way to go. A tall black figure in a fine blue shirt stepped out of the shadows and flashed a pearly smile at her. She remembered seeing him when she arrived.

'Hello,' she said uncertainly, 'I'm afraid I'm lost.'

He grinned even more broadly. He was big and handsome with a powerfully built body.

'You are Miss Merrill?' he enquired politely and she nodded. 'I am William. I work for Mister Morgan.'

His English was surprisingly good. Lexi took his outstretched hand and shook it.

'Where is everybody?' she asked, and he pointed towards a long, dimly-lit passageway.

'Down there and turn to the right. They are on the terrace with their iced drinks and their diamonds . . . ' He spoke with a hint of bitterness, then turned to her apologetically. 'So sorry, Miss Merrill. I should not have said that. Mister Morgan and Miss Belle, they are waiting for you to join them. Please, have a good evening. I will see you tomorrow, perhaps.'

'Perhaps. Thank you. Goodnight, William.'

Lexi stood hesitantly in the arched doorway that opened out on to the cool, marble-tiled terrace. The air was heady with perfume. It was already dusk and a white jacketed servant was busily lighting an array of antique oil lamps that glowed pink, lending a romantic ambiance to the already exotic setting.

The first person she recognised was Rusty, looking incredibly young and attractive. He was talking with great animation to a middle-aged couple whom she took to be the Bensons. The man was overweight and looked uncomfortable in his evening jacket and stiff bow tie. His wife, some years younger, was expensively dressed, her robust figure thrust into a Paris model in dark sage taffeta. As William had indicated, she was dripping in diamonds and flashing a huge diamond and emerald ring with over-exaggerated theatrical movements of her left hand.

Morgan Tyler stood a few feet away, tall and ruggedly handsome. He was in the process of handing out drinks to two young women, one the beautiful Christine, who was the Benson's daughter. She was dressed in a red chiffon top and white trousers The other, younger girl, was almost drab by comparison, in a modest blue denim skirt and broderie anglaise top.

The arrival of Lexi in their midst seemed to distract Morgan slightly, to the extent that he spilled the drink he was handing to Christine, which made her cry out a sharp warning. However, it was Lexi everybody turned to look at as she went on to the terrace.

Rusty looked embarrassed and quickly downed his drink, then strode over to the bar to replenish it. Mr and Mrs Benson eyed Lexi with some curiosity, but made no effort to come forward to greet her. Both the younger women seemed to resent her presence.

'Ah, Lexi, there you are!' Belle came to her rescue, bearing down on her, floating along in a cool African cotton Kaftan in varying shades of brown and amber, set off with numerous strings of ethnic beads. 'Come and give me a hand, will you? It's such a lovely evening, we've decided to eat out here. I'll introduce you to the Bensons later. My girl Maria is in a flap because there's been a change of plan. Just check that she's laid out the table correctly, will you, while I sort out the food in the kitchen.'

'Yes, of course.' Lexi was glad of an excuse not to join the others.

* * *

'Well, this is a turn up for the books, isn't it!' She turned to find Rusty. He appeared to be a little the worse for wear, judging by the way he swayed slightly.

'Hello, Rusty,' Lexi said.

'This isn't exactly what I had planned for us,' he said, gulping down yet another drink. 'Lexi, what can I say?'

'Don't say anything, Rusty. I think that would be best, don't you?'

'Seeing the way you look tonight . . . ' Rusty put out his hand and gripped her shoulder. ' . . . I might change my mind again. Maybe . . . '

'I think Belle would like your help in the kitchen, Rusty.'

They both jumped at the sudden intrusion of Morgan Tyler's voice, sailing clear across the terrace. Leaving Bobbie and Christine, he strolled across to Lexi and Rusty. For just a moment Rusty stood his ground, then pushed past his brother and left the room on unsteady legs.

'Good evening,' Morgan said to Lexi. 'I was beginning to think you weren't going to join us.'

'I'm afraid your stepmother and I got a little carried away and then I took longer than necessary to shower and change.' Lexi turned her attention back to the cutlery, moving knives and forks about unnecessarily just for something to do.

'Belle likes you. That's a mark in your favour. She doesn't take easily to strangers as a rule. What did you do, spike her whisky?'

'That's unfair!' Lexi flashed at him, then realised he was smiling; the remark had been meant as a joke.

'Let's see if we can get through our first evening without drawing swords, shall we?' He kept his voice low so that only she could hear him.

'I have no intention of sparring with

71

you, Mr Tyler,' she said, casting a glance over her shoulder and flushing with embarrassment as she found every pair of eyes in the room directed at her.

'That's very wise of you.' Morgan observed the other occupants of the terrace. 'I'd say, judging from the reaction of the present company, you're going to need all the friendly support you can get. Besides, no-one ever spars with me with the intention of winning.'

Lexi started to object to this remark, but was silenced by his raised voice and his fingers clamped around her arm.

'A drink, Lexi! How remiss of me! What will you have? White wine, I think, yes?'

'Thank you.' She nodded and watched as he strode over to the drinks trolley and poured her a drink, then brought it back, presenting it to her with a flourish and a glint in those amazing eyes of his.

'Thank you.' She took a grateful sip from the chilled liquid and said as an aside, 'I had no idea I was so transparent!'

'I beg your pardon?'

'White wine! You seemed to have no difficulty deciding what I wanted without my even mentioning it. Are you a mind reader, or don't you think women are entitled to a mind of their own?'

He frowned down at her, the muscles of his jawline taut.

'You're in a stressful situation and you're unaccustomed to this heat,' he said. 'Anything stronger than that stuff could have adverse effects. I wouldn't want to have to pick you up and carry you off like a little girl who's had too much to drink.'

'Carrying me off, conscious or otherwise, is something you'll never get to experience, I assure you!'

Lexi tossed back her head and gulped down her wine, but the jerkiness of her self-conscious action made her spill it. She stood there, feeling ridiculous, wine dripping down her chin, as she turned her back on the room and fumbled for her handkerchief. Not finding one, she put down her glass and stumbled off the terrace, down the spreading fan of marble steps and into the dark, velvety African night.

★   ★   ★

The ground was rough beneath her feet as she walked as far as she dared from the glowing terrace and the tinkling female conversation punctuated by beefy guffaws of laughter from Mr Benson. The soft, warm air was filled with the chirping of cicadas. Somewhere there was a plop, then a splash, that told her there must be water close by. A low grunting off to the right followed by a distant throaty rumbling roar made her stop abruptly and swing round as leaves rustled and a twig cracked close behind her. As she moved, her sleeve caught on a spiny thorn tree branch. She gave a little gasp and tugged, but the material held fast.

A low, amused laugh startled her still further and she stood there, panting and staring blindly into the darkness.

'You look like a frightened impala.' Morgan Tyler was suddenly beside her again. 'Here, hold still. These thorns are lethal. It's a wonder you didn't do yourself more damage rushing out into the dark like that. This isn't England, you know. For a start, we have snakes here, as well as thorn trees.'

As he talked, he worked on the trapped fabric of her dress. She could only half see him in the dusk, but as he put his arms about her, the better to deal with the tenacious thorns, she felt her body melt and sway uncontrollably towards him, as if drawn by a powerful magnet.

Just as her sleeve came free, there was another strange, reverberating growl, closer this time. Lexi caught her breath and gave an involuntary jump forward. It placed her up against Morgan's broad chest and, surprisingly, she could feel his heart beating through the thin silk of his shirt. The beats drummed against her ribcage where her own heart was fluttering like a captive butterfly.

'What was that?' she asked and her voice caught in her throat.

'What?' He hesitated, his arms around her, his eyes searching her face, just visible in the moonlight; not cold eyes in that fleeting moment, but troubled, confused eyes. His lips were close to her forehead and she could feel his warm breath disturbing a wisp of hair that had fallen out of place. 'Oh, that! It was a lioness. Hunting probably. They come pretty close at night. Another reason for not wandering off on your own.'

Neither of them had moved. Morgan's arms still held her and he showed no desire to remove them. On the contrary, he pulled her closer. She felt sure he was going to kiss her and while she told herself she should be objecting loudly to such treatment from her ex-fiancé's brother, as his head came down towards hers, she knew she would welcome his kiss.

Then he snapped upright suddenly and pushed himself away from her. 'Little fool!' His words lashed out cruelly, chafing at her senses.

'What?'

'You! Rusty! This whole business! Let's go back before they start getting any wrong ideas about us.'

'Heaven forbid!' she retaliated.

★ ★ ★

As they reached the steps to the terrace, Lexi caught a glimpse of red chiffon and Christine's face, pale with anger, eyes dark and accusing. Mrs Benson was busily patting her daughter's hand and asking what the trouble was. The girl shook her head vigorously and led the way to the table, where Belle was waiting patiently.

'Ah, there you are, you two!' Belle beamed and ushered Lexi into the seat next to her own. 'Has Morgan been showing you around? I hope he remembered to tell you never to wander about out here alone at night. There have been incidences with lions getting into the enclosure, but we haven't lost a guest yet!'

'And we would hate to start with you, Lexi,' Morgan sat down opposite Lexi and flashed her a smile she couldn't quite fathom.

'Oh, I don't know.' Christine, with an expression something akin to a snake about to strike, came up behind Morgan's chair. She slid her arms about his neck and kissed his cheek. 'I've been wandering around this place all my life and nothing terrible has ever happened to me!'

She slithered into the chair next to Morgan and placed a hand on his arm, her eyes flashing a message of possession across the table to Lexi.

'There isn't a creature out there, my pet, who would dare take you on,' Morgan retorted, then took her hand and firmly removed it from his arm. 'Besides, you must remember that Lexi is a stranger here and not used either to our customs or the strange animals that prowl in the night . . . or in the daytime, for that matter.'

'Has anybody seen Rusty?' Belle's voice interrupted impatiently and Lexi was grateful to have the attention turned to someone else.

'I'll look for him!' The girl, Bobbie, jumped up, and, throwing aside her napkin, hurriedly left the room before Belle could stop her.

'Oh, that girl! What is wrong with her?' Belle shook her head.

'Adolescence. Some children can't really cope with it, you know.' Mrs Benson rattled the diamonds around her neck and smiled benevolently at her daughter. 'It's such a traumatic time for them.'

'It seems to me that some of them never grow out of it,' Morgan remarked pointedly, eyeing Lexi across the table. Far from amusing her, it merely served to increase the irritation that was boiling inside her.

'I don't remember adolescence making me as jumpy as a cricket,' Belle laughed. 'Nor do I remember being depressed. In fact, I sometimes think I jumped from childhood to womanhood in one giant leap, but then I suppose it was necessary for me to grow up pretty quickly.'

'Were you born here, Belle?' Lexi asked, for something to say. 'You don't look English ... I mean ... ' She floundered and was rewarded with a warm, friendly smile.

'I know what you mean, dear,' Belle said. 'Yes, I was born here, but my father was a Polish immigrant, a poor, simple peasant, but honest and hard-working. Unfortunately, he discovered whisky long before he was able to make his mark in this country.'

As if in mock tribute to alcohol, Belle raised her own glass and drained it, receiving a look of disapproval from Morgan which did not go unnoticed, for she grimaced back at him, then reached out and gave his cheek a motherly pat.

'And your mother?' Lexi went on,

'was she Polish, too?'

There was a sudden silence. Belle and Morgan exchanged glances and although the older woman did not blush, she looked decidedly uncomfortable.

'My mother was . . . she was born here . . . ' Belle answered and turned her attention to the sound of approaching footsteps. She breathed an obvious sigh of relief at the sight of Rusty, slightly dishevelled, being escorted on to the terrace by a determined Bobbie. 'Ah, thank goodness. Now, perhaps, we can get on with dinner. Come on, you two. Where was he, Bobbie? Never mind! He's here now. Let's eat, shall we?'

The meal was delicious, but Lexi had little appetite. She found her mind wandering back to that moment out there in the darkness and her close encounter with Morgan. She felt her cheeks colour, convinced that her thoughts must be written across her forehead in flashing neon signs for everybody to see.

She had come so close to making an utter and absolute fool of herself. She had wanted Morgan to kiss her. A man she hardly knew, didn't even like. A man who had made it painfully clear that he despised her.

It shouldn't matter to her that he had her figured out all wrong, but it did. It mattered a great deal.

Lexi looked up and was startled to find Morgan staring at her with an intensity that made her throat constrict. For what seemed a long time, their eyes were locked together, then he blinked and focused his attention on Harry Benson who was asking some advice about stock market shares.

'Are you all right, dear?' Belle touched Lexi's arm, making her jump as if she'd been stung.

'Oh, Belle, I'm sorry. I was miles away!'

'You haven't eaten much. Don't you feel well?'

'Oh, no; everything was delicious. It's

just . . . I . . . ' Lexi spread her hands.

'It's probably the heat. You're not used to it. It takes a while to adjust.'

'Yes,' Lexi smiled gratefully at her hostess. 'Belle, would you think it unsociable of me to excuse myself? I feel awfully tired suddenly and, well, I think perhaps things are catching up with me.'

'Not at all, dear! All in all, it's been quite a day for you. You'll feel much better for a night's rest. We'll talk in the morning about what you're going to do while you're here with us.'

'You're very kind.' Lexi got to her feet. 'I don't deserve all this.'

'Nonsense! Now, off you go to bed and we'll see you in the morning.'

Lexi said goodnight, then walked wearily across the terrace. She felt as if her body and her mind were gripped in a kind of exhaustion. Jet-lag, unaccustomed heat and emotional upheavals had all joined forces and were wearing her down.

Then, halfway down the main hall,

an all-engulfing blackness crept up on her and all feeling went out of her body. She felt herself move as if floating on air, then her shoulder came up against the hard wall and she seemed to be clutching blindly at nothing while trying desperately not to pass out.

'Lean against me!' Morgan's voice sounded distant and strangely echoing.

'I'm awfully sorry,' she heard herself say, in the same echoing voice that sounded miles away. 'I think I'm going to faint.'

★　★　★

She couldn't tell how long she was out, but when she came to, he was carrying her up the stairs and along the corridor in the direction of her bedroom.

'What are you doing?' she demanded weakly and stupidly, since it was patently obvious what he was doing.

'I'm doing exactly what you told me two hours ago that I would never get to do,' he said flatly. 'I'm carrying you off.'

'Please put me down!'

'Don't be ridiculous. If I put you down right now you'd likely fall and do yourself an injury. I'm not willing to risk that, even if you are.'

'Of course not! I'd hate to think I had to stay here any longer than is necessary.'

'Then keep still and shut up.' He kicked open the door to her room, carried her in and laid her on the bed with surprising gentleness.

'I really don't think . . . ' She started to struggle up into a sitting position but found that the room was tilting at a precarious angle.

'Lie back and take it easy.' He pushed her back against the pillows and held her there until he was sure she wasn't going to disobey him, then he moved to the foot of the bed and she felt him remove her sandals.

She could feel the darkness engulfing her again. This time, she allowed it to happen. Tomorrow, when she woke up, it would be a new day, and the impossible dream she was dreaming right now would be gone forever.

★  ★  ★

There was a swish of a curtain as someone pulled it along the rail and a blinding light as the morning sun streamed into the room, falling mercilessly on Lexi's face. She groaned and shaded her eyes, then remembered with a shock that she was not back home in England, but still in Kenya.

The memory of the previous evening flashed through her brain like a fire bolt and jolted her awake.

A second curtain was dragged back noisily by a vigorous hand.

'Good morning!'

The girl, Bobbie, dressed in the same blue denim skirt she had worn last night, was standing by the window.

'I brought you some orange juice.' Bobbie's thin, tomboy-ish face was unsmiling and the dark eyes held the same brooding stare Lexi had noticed at dinner the evening before.

'That's very kind of you.'

Bobbie shrugged and half turned to look out of the window, although she seemed to be staring into space, reluctant to meet Lexi's eyes and yet just as reluctant to leave.

'It was Belle's idea,' she said.

'Well, thank you for bringing it anyway.'

The thin shoulders rose and fell again. 'I wanted to see you . . . talk to you . . . ' A quick glance at Lexi, then the almond-shaped eyes returned to the middle distance outside the window.

'What did you want to talk about?' Lexi said kindly.

Long slender fingers combed nervously through the short-cropped black hair, then the hands were stuffed self-consciously into the deep pockets of the denim skirt.

'It's difficult,' Bobbie said.

Lexi studied the girl's profile, deciding that it wouldn't take much to turn her into an extremely beautiful young woman. In profile she looked amazingly similar to the black ebony Maasai bust standing in an alcove in the main hall. There were the same fine contours, the same proud tilt to the head. She was light skinned, but with an olive tinge that spoke of mixed parentage.

'Perhaps it could wait until I'm up and dressed?' Lexi suggested.

'No!' The girl spun around and faced her. 'I have to talk to you now. If I wait . . . well, things will get all out of hand . . . '

'Bobbie, what is it that bothers you about me?' Lexi took a grateful sip of orange juice and looked at the girl. 'It's obvious that you dislike me for some reason, but I haven't the faintest notion why, since we hadn't met before last night. In fact, before last night, I didn't even know you existed, so I can hardly have done anything to upset you. Now, don't you think you owe me some kind of explanation so that I can at least defend myself?'

Bobbie nodded in agreement and her

eyes seemed to fill with unshed tears, but she hid them from Lexi and talked down to the polished wood block floor.

'I thought everything was going to be all right when they said the engagement was off . . . you and Rusty, I mean.'

'The engagement is off, Bobbie! Actually, it was never really on.'

'But you came anyway. You would have married him!'

'Actually, I don't think I would have. I was already beginning to have doubts and now, seeing Rusty again, I'm quite sure that if he hadn't broken it off, I would have.'

'He didn't break off the engagement! Morgan did!'

'Morgan?' Lexi struggled to make sense of this sudden revelation.

'Yes. He told Rusty he was making a big mistake. They had quite a fight over it. But Morgan won. Morgan always wins. Don't get me wrong. He was right to do what he did. He usually is. He's marvellous. It's just, well, Rusty took it badly. Then he seemed to get over it and I thought . . . I hoped . . . But then you came here and Rusty is hurting and I can't bear to see him hurting and . . . But he wouldn't be happy married to you. He doesn't love you, not really. And you don't love him, so neither of you would be happy, so why don't you go away and leave us alone!'

So that was it. The poor girl was in love with Rusty, but the love she had for him was unrequited, the most painful kind of all. Rusty probably didn't even know she existed outside the superficial, brother-sister relationship they had built up over the years.

'Oh, Bobbie, I'm so sorry!' Lexi, clutching her sheet around her, swung her legs out of the bed and padded across the Indian rug to stand face to face with the girl. She put a sympathetic hand on Bobbie's shoulder and the dark eyes stared up into hers, full of sadness. 'Bobbie, I don't want to hurt anyone. Rusty and I were both in a silly, foolish mood when we met back in England. We got carried away, briefly.

Mistaken emotions can cause all sorts of havoc.

'But you can rest assured that anything there might have been between us was pretty shallow and it was over almost before it began. I now feel very humiliated and ashamed that I let it happen.

'I think Rusty probably feels that way, too.'

'If he doesn't love you, then why is he hurting so much? He won't speak to me, won't let me anywhere near him. And we used to be such good friends.'

'I don't know, Bobbie. Maybe he's confused and angry. Maybe he resents his older brother telling him how to live his life, so he's trying to prove something to Morgan. I only know that I have no intention of staying here. Just as soon as the strike is over, I'm catching the first flight out . . . alone.'

Bobbie turned away and hastily scrubbed at a tear.

'I thought . . . ' She gave a hiccupping sob. 'I thought you were the same as Christine, but you're not, are you?'

'The same as Christine?'

'Yes. We used to be good friends, but . . . well, all she can think of is how she can trap Morgan into marrying her. She's always been crazy about him, ever since she was a little girl. I don't think she would be right for him, but Christine has a habit of getting what she wants, one way or another. What her father can't buy for her, she begs, borrows or steals.'

'It sounds as if Morgan and Christine would be perfect for one another,' Lexi remarked, and received a disapproving look from Bobbie.

'If you knew Morgan at all, you wouldn't say that, Morgan is the most wonderful person in the world!'

'Well,' Lexi sighed, 'I'm afraid there isn't going to be time for me to get to know the Morgan Tyler you describe.'

'No, I suppose not. Lexi, I'm sorry I was rotten to you. I think we could be friends, you and I . . . if you stayed around long enough.'

Lexi smiled warmly at her and Bobbie grinned back. 'I bet you were surprised to wake up this morning without your clothes!' she laughed.

'I'm afraid I don't remember anything after I got into bed.'

'It was Belle who settled you. When Morgan came and told her you'd passed out, she couldn't rest until she'd made you comfortable.'

'She's a nice lady,' Lexi murmured gratefully.

'We're all nice, really, if you take the time to get to know us.'

Yes, Lexi thought. It was always a matter of time. Waiting for the right time, not rushing headlong into situations before giving oneself time. And now, in a few days, she would say her goodbyes. It was no time at all.

But something was telling her that it would take her a long time to forget the Tylers; Belle, Rusty, Bobbie, Morgan. Especially Morgan.

# Christine Puts Lexi in Danger

The voices on the terrace were lowered and almost masked by the clatter of cutlery and crockery, but the tone was unmistakably argumentative and just a little heated. Lexi's sandals clacking on the tiled floor heralded her approach, but just in case her arrival went unnoticed, she cleared her throat and said a breezy 'Good Morning!' to the shy black girl called Maria, who was squeezing fresh oranges into a large crystal jug.

'*Jambo, bi!*' the girl replied with a smile.

Belle and Morgan were seated at the table. It was they who had been arguing. Their conversation came to an abrupt end as they looked across to where Lexi stood uncertainly. Belle waved her over with a welcoming smile, while Morgan, grim-faced, poured himself another cup of coffee.

'How do you feel this morning, my dear?' Belle asked.

'I feel fine, thank you. I'm sorry to be a nuisance.'

'You weren't! You were exhausted, and I don't wonder that everything got on top of you.'

Belle indicated the chair next to hers and Lexi sat down. 'I've been trying to persuade Morgan to take some time off and treat you to a safari trip while you're here,' Belle told her, 'but he seems to think there are certain things that can't be put off.' She turned to him. 'Morgan, surely you can rearrange your schedule, especially since the group you were expecting have cancelled because of the strike.'

'I can't get out of this one, Belle.' Morgan stared down into his cup. 'It's taken a long time to set up the meeting with the Kastner Brothers and I know there's some big American organisation wanting in on the deal. You know what will happen if they buy the Kastner property. It'll be Fun City in the bush. I've heard they're even thinking of importing animatronic wild animals so their guests can shoot them with blank cartridges. It'll be just like Disneyland.'

'But that's terrible!' Lexi's outburst was spontaneous and when Morgan glanced across at her, she coloured and fell silent.

'There, you see, Belle!' he said, 'even Lexi can see how important this meeting is, and she doesn't know the first thing about it.'

'I'm sorry,' Lexi said, 'I didn't mean to talk out of turn, but it does seem like sacrilege to bring in stuffed or plastic animals when there are so many beautiful animals roaming around live out here. And I don't think guns should be encouraged. I mean . . . well, you can't let them do it!'

Morgan was watching Lexi intently. For the first time, she thought, he neither looked sarcastic nor indifferent, but interested, as if he'd discovered a real person beneath the outer shell that was Lexi Merrill.

'Let me make a phone call,' he said, getting up. 'Maybe we can work something out that will be beneficial all round.'

As he walked out, Belle reached over and squeezed Lexi's hand. There was a mischievous glint in her eyes and a dimple in the wide smile that still spoke of youth and vitality. She was the type of woman, Lexi decided, who would still have the power to attract and to charm, even in her old age.

★ ★ ★

They had finished breakfast by the time Morgan returned. He didn't look very hopeful. 'It's no good, I'm afraid. They have to come to Nairobi on other business. I couldn't persuade them to hold our meeting at Amboseli instead.'

'Ah, that's too bad!' Belle shook her head.

Lexi smiled through a slow surge of disappointment. It might have been fun going on safari with Morgan, she mused. Oh well, you couldn't alter your own fate, and it seemed that her fate was not to get to know the man any better than she did right now.

'I've been in touch with William and he's agreed to come in on his day off,' Morgan was saying.

'Oh, yes,' Lexi nodded. 'I met him last night on the way to dinner. He seemed angry about something.'

Morgan gave a short laugh. 'That was the Bensons, I'm afraid. They're out-and-out snobs and think nothing of insulting people like William. In their eyes, anyone who wasn't born of true-blood English stock and hasn't had a University education isn't worth the time of day. William doesn't take kindly to that kind of treatment. Neither do I.'

'Harry Benson was Morgan's father's best friend, and their fathers before them were pretty close, so we sort of inherited them,' Belle explained. 'It's a very dubious inheritance, as I keep telling Morgan, but he's too nice to cut himself off from them.'

'I can see how difficult that would be,' Lexi said, thinking of Christine Benson. She folded her napkin, careful not to look at Morgan, but feeling his eyes on her. 'Anyway,' he said, 'William is coming over from Nairobi and he's going to take you out on a short safari.'

'That's very kind, really, but you don't have to put yourselves out for me. I mean, it's my fault, after all, that you've been lumbered with me. I can just as easily find a quiet corner and read a book.'

'You'll do no such thing, my girl, and if anyone should take the blame, it's Rusty,' Belle said. 'You go out with William. He's a good man. He'll look after you.'

'But I feel so guilty. After all, it is his day off.'

'Oh, believe me, he volunteered,' Morgan said. 'He said if it was for you, he would gladly give up his free time.

What did you say to him last night? He was very impressed.'

Lexi locked eyes with Morgan. Doing her best to ignore the fluttering in her stomach, she smiled serenely at him. 'It may surprise you to know that some people don't find it too difficult to like me.'

'I'll make a note of that for future reference. Now, if you'll excuse me, William will be here in an hour. Belle will advise you on what to wear.'

Belle was looking from one to the other with a perplexed frown, and as soon as Morgan was out of earshot she turned to Lexi. 'What was that all about?'

'Oh, nothing, Belle.' Lexi shrugged and gave a sigh of resignation. 'Morgan doesn't exactly approve of me, and I can't say I blame him, really. After all, I hardly knew Rusty when I agreed to come out here and marry him. Oh, Belle, I was such a fool, wasn't I!'

'We're all fools at some stage in our lives . . . some of us more so than others. Anyway, Morgan is in no position to criticise you. He did much the same thing when he was Rusty's age, only he didn't have a big brother around to save him. Morgan married his mistake and learned from it the hard way. He's still paying, unfortunately. What he needs is another woman to help him forget.'

'I should think he could have any woman he wants.'

'He could, but he doesn't want just 'any' woman. He's looking for that one special person, and that's not easy when you're a Tyler man. They're all red-blooded and a little too headstrong for their own good. Rusty's open with his emotions. Morgan keeps his hidden. I'm not sure whether to envy the woman who finally gets to his heart, or feel sorry her.'

'Christine certainly seems to be working on it!'

'Christine's just a silly spoiled child. Don't worry yourself about Christine, Lexi. Morgan's no fool any more when it comes to women. He won't make a second mistake, believe me.'

'I'm not at all worried about him. Why should I be? After all, it's got nothing to do with me.'

'Hmm.' There was that knowing smile again. 'Come on, let's see what clothes you've got that will be suitable for this mini-safari.'

★ ★ ★

As it happened, William rang an hour later, full of apologies, to say that his jeep had broken down. There was no way he could get out to Redlands in time to take Lexi on safari.

'It seems I'm not meant to see the country after all,' Lexi said when Belle brought her the news.

'Never mind, dear,' Belle sympathised, 'there's always tomorrow. I happen to know that Morgan has no plans for the rest of the week. I'm sure he'll be the perfect guide.'

'Who'll be the perfect guide?'

They looked up to see Christine Benson sauntering towards them, slinky in yellow silk shirt, matching headband and riding breeches.

'Well, good morning, young lady!' Belle gave a tight smile that said she wasn't too pleased to see the girl, but was doing her best to hide the fact. 'Hasn't your father persuaded you to go back to University yet?'

Christine gave a derisive snort and tossed her head. 'I've never known my father able to make me do anything I don't want to.'

'You're wasting such a lot, Christine. You'll regret it later.'

'You sound like Morgan. Speaking of whom, where is he? I thought we'd go riding this morning.'

'Morgan is attending a very important meeting in Nairobi. Goodness, girl, he's a very busy man. You can't expect him to be available at any given time just because you want him. He has a business to run.'

Christine's face clouded and her

mouth turned down into a petulant pout. 'He doesn't have to be so busy all the time! According to Rusty, the business practically runs itself.'

'I would hardly take Rusty's word for it,' Belle said. 'He's never been at Redlands long enough to know anything about the business. He's too busy leading the life of a playboy.'

'Oh, I'm sorry, Belle!' Christine suddenly became ingratiating, possibly realising that it wouldn't do to get on the wrong side of this powerful, all-important member of the Tyler family. 'But I am annoyed with Morgan. The least he can do is spend some time with me while I'm here. It's not too much to ask, is it?'

'Perhaps it is,' Belle said. 'Maybe you should find someone else to play with.'

'I would, but this place is deserted. I couldn't even find Bobbie, not that she's much company. Where are they all, anyway?'

'They're all in Nairobi.' Belle busied herself piling the breakfast dishes on a tray. 'Morgan's at a meeting, Rusty's doing whatever Rusty does in Nairobi, and Bobbie is at Secretarial College trying desperately to make something of herself.'

Christine gave a sarcastic sneer. 'I should think that's a losing battle! I mean, she's not exactly over-endowed with beauty or brains, is she? I doubt she'll ever be anything other than a witless frump.'

At that last remark, Lexi decided it was time she joined in the conversation, although Christine had done a remarkably good job so far of ignoring her presence.

'That's unfair,' she said sharply and the other girl blinked in surprise. 'Bobbie's still very young. She may be a little gauche, but she's basically a very nice girl. Good looks aren't everything, Christine. Besides, I think Bobbie could be very attractive. Perhaps, instead of criticising her, you should be helping her to discover her best assets.'

'Personally, I don't think she has any,

but what business is it of yours? You're just a stranger here. An interloper.'

'Christine!' Belle banged a cup and saucer down on the table and swung around to face her young visitor. 'If you are going to be insulting to Lexi, I suggest you leave right now. And, just for the record, when you were only a little younger than Bobbie, you were overweight, spotty, pug-nosed and given to tantrums. Well, you lost a few pounds, got rid of the spots and had your nose fixed, but as far as I'm concerned, you're still the same underneath and one day someone is going to teach you a lesson you won't forget. Now, if you'll excuse me, I have work to do. If you want to do something to help, you could show Lexi around Redlands, since her day out has been postponed.'

Christine bristled angrily, and then a sudden calm seemed to come over her. 'Well, why not! I don't suppose you ride, do you?'

Lexi started to decline the offer. She

had taken only a few riding lessons when she was fifteen, followed by a humiliating pony trekking holiday the year after. She hadn't been near a horse since.

'Well, do you ride?' Christine asked impatiently.

'Yes, of course,' Lexi heard herself saying. 'But it's some time since I was on a horse.'

'It's no different to riding a bike. Once you've learned how you never forget. Come on.'

'Well, I . . . '

'Look, are you coming or not? I'm getting bored with this place. I imagine you feel pretty much the same, having been dumped so publicly.'

'Well, it wasn't exactly like that, but . . . all right . . . ' Lexi wished Belle would come up with some reason why she shouldn't go. However, Belle simply nodded her approval and hurried out of the room with a brief wave of her hand and an instruction to, 'have a good day.'

'Don't worry,' Christine said, as she led the way across the wide courtyard towards the stables where Lexi could see the girl's black stallion tethered, 'you can take Mbaya. She's Morgan's horse, but he won't mind. You'll be all right with her. See! There she is, already saddled, since I expected Morgan to be coming with me.'

Lexi followed Christine's pointing finger and saw a young stable boy leading a huge grey mare across the enclosure. It was bigger than Christine's mount and had a powerful, muscular build. Its proud head was held high and it was pulling at the reins, which the boy was having difficulty hanging on to. The long, flowing, creamy-white mane and tail glistened silvery in the morning sunshine.

'She's beautiful,' Lexi said, swallowing her fear and trying to put a brave face on what could turn out to be a gross mistake on her part. Another idiotic act for Morgan to add to his growing list.

'She looks awesome, doesn't she, but she's a pussycat, really. Matthew! Help Miss Merrill to mount,' Christine said, and swung herself into her own saddle with the ease of an athlete.

Lexi closed her eyes and took a few deep breaths while the stable boy waited for the moment she would step into his cupped hands so that he could hoist her up.

'You okay, *bi*?' Matthew, the stable-boy, said a little uncertainly as he got ready to take her weight. 'Mbaya don't like to be kept waiting, Miss Merrill. You sure you want to ride her?'

'No, I'm not sure, Matthew,' Lexi whispered, with a glance over her shoulder to where Christine and her horse were pacing about, eager to get going. 'But I'm going to, anyway.'

She stepped into the boy's cupped hands and suddenly she was flying up into the air, one leg going over the horse's back, both hands clutching desperately at the saddle. She landed heavily, but somehow managed to stay on, thinking how much easier it must be for Morgan to sit astride the animal because of his long legs.

Matthew quickly adjusted the stirrups and handed her the reins. He looked anything but happy. 'Mr Morgan, he say it okay for you to ride Mbaya?' he asked cautiously.

'Mr Morgan doesn't know. Miss Christine said he wouldn't mind.'

'Oh!' Matthew looked at Christine, now trotting off into the distance, then back at Lexi, and shook his head. 'You take care, *bi*. She fast. You want to go slow, you say, *pole-pole*, Mbaya. Don't shout, just say softly *pole-pole*. Okay, *bi*?'

'Thank you, Matthew.' Lexi gripped the reins and gently urged the big mare forward as the boy stepped back, shaking his head and muttering to himself.

The mare was more than ready to be off and broke into an immediate canter as it rushed to catch up to the black stallion. There was a shout from Matthew and the horse slowed to a more comfortable trot.

'What kept you?' Christine said, as they drew up beside her.

'Just exchanging a few words with Matthew,' Lexi said a little breathlessly, relieved that her horse was now happily falling into step with the black stallion.

'What did he say to you?' Christine asked suspiciously.

'Nothing much, just a few words of advice.'

'Such as?'

'Oh, he told me what to say to make Mbaya slow down, but . . . ' Lexi realised suddenly that in her nervousness she had already forgotten the instruction.'

'The boy is a fool, they're all fools. He probably told you the wrong word just to get you into trouble.'

'So it's not sufficient to just say 'whoa'?' Lexi smiled, in order to show that she was joking. She was beginning to enjoy herself, now that she had overcome her initial fear. It was exhilarating sitting on such a magnificent animal.

Christine gave a derisive laugh. 'Morgan prefers to use Swahili with the animals. He's so good with them. Well, he's so good with everything. And he's especially good at attracting women.' Christine must have seen Lexi's expression change at this remark, and her smile widened as she pressed on. 'I bet you felt something the first time you looked into those eyes of his, didn't you?'

'Don't be silly, Christine!' Lexi could feel a flush of embarrassment creep up from her neck. She turned her head away to look at the scenery in the hope that Christine wouldn't notice.

'It's not just his eyes, though, is it? It's everything about him. He's magnificent, don't you think?'

'I really don't want to talk about Morgan. I hardly know the man.

Anyway, I'll be going back to England very shortly.'

'That's good. Because you see, Morgan's mine. He's always been mine, whether he admits it or not. Haven't you noticed how he is when he's near me?'

'I've noticed he gets rather irritable!'

'That's just his way of hiding his true feelings. I have to wait for the right moment and then . . . ' She threw back her head and laughed. 'Believe me, Lexi, he'll be putty in my hands.'

Lexi shuddered. She didn't want to hear talk like this, not about Morgan. So far, everything Christine had said had plunged inside Lexi like a knife, leaving a dull pain. How very, very strange.

Come on, Lexi, you fool, she admonished silently as they rode on together. What difference does it make to you if Christine sets out to get Morgan? You'll soon be thousands of miles away and you'll forget him once you get your life back on track.

★   ★   ★

'Blast!' Christine pulled up sharply and her horse reared as it felt the sharp bite of the bit in its sensitive mouth.

'What's wrong?' Mbaya danced nervously and Lexi had difficulty controlling her.

'I had a message for Belle about this evening and I forgot to give it to her. It's important. I'd better go back.'

'I'll come with you.' Lexi felt she had had enough riding for one day, and was glad of an excuse to return to the house, but Christine shook her head.

'No. It won't take me more than five minutes if I ride hard. I know a short-cut. You go on. I'll catch you up. Just follow the road. You can't go wrong.'

'Well, I'm not sure that I . . . '

'Lexi! Don't be such a wimp!'

'Tell me again how I slow Mbaya down?'

Christine gave a long, loud sigh. 'You're really not much of a rider, are you? It's a good job Morgan isn't here. He doesn't have much time for people who don't ride. He taught me when I was two.'

'The command, Christine, please?'

'Oh, yes . . . sorry . . . *haraka* . . . Just shout *haraka* loudly and she'll slow down.'

'I'm sure that wasn't the word Matthew told me to say . . . and he said to speak softly, not to shout . . . '

'Matthew is a trouble-maker. He no doubt thinks it's funny to give you the wrong instructions. He's been in trouble recently with Morgan and this is probably his way of getting back at him.'

'So, I shout *haraka*?'

'That's right. Good and loud. She responds to firm handling. Otherwise, she'll just go her own way. Look, I'm off. Won't be long.'

In a choking cloud of red dust, the black stallion galloped away, leaving the mare jittery and dancing on the spot. Nervously, Lexi tried to move her forward, but Mbaya didn't respond, so Lexi squeezed her legs round the horse's girth, gently at first, and then more firmly.

The horse jumped about, whinnying and snorting, then took off at a wild gallop, but in the wrong direction. Lexi gasped and grabbed hold of the thick mane in one hand as she struggled with the reins in the other.

'Mbaya!' she shouted, half screaming at the horse in her panic. 'Mbaya! *Haraka! Haraka!*'

Instead of slowing down, the grey picked up speed and soon Lexi was clinging on for dear life, lying half prone across the pommel which was beating a bruising tattoo against her ribs. The red earth sped by a few feet beneath her. Dust and stones were being kicked up in the wake of those pounding hoofs.

Lexi struggled to sit up, but the jolting speed at which they were travelling made it impossible. She felt herself losing her grip. A quick glance ahead showed that the horse had left the rough track and was heading for a low wire fence.

She cried out, her voice rough with fearful anticipation, sure that they would crash into the wires. In that split second, the one thought that flashed through her numbed brain was the fact that Morgan would never forgive her this last act of foolishness.

One minute the fence was there, looming menacingly in front of them. The next minute, horse and rider were flying high above the wires. Lexi's feet had long-since lost their hold in the stirrups and now the reins had gone and the long strands of mane were-sliding through her fingers. She felt herself lift from the saddle and there was nothing beneath her except a red blur.

She hit the ground and rolled over and over down a shallow ravine, her fall cushioned by clumps of spiky bush scrub. As she came to a halt, she could hear the fading sound of Mbaya's pounding hoofs disappearing into the distance.

With a groan, she tried to sit up, but everything hurt so much she thought she would just lie there for a while.

The sun beat down mercilessly as she drifted in and out of a kind of semi-conscious state. It was a sound close to her right ear that made her raise her head painfully and squint about her. There it was again, a soft rustling in the dry grass a few feet away. Then she saw it. A large snake was making slow, slithering progress in her direction.

Lexi froze. The snake stopped and almost immediately it seemed to disappear, its camouflage colours blending in with its background. Then it moved again and she saw that its eyes were fixed on her. She wanted to move, but she couldn't. She was paralysed with fear.

Then a quiet whistling sound passed close to her ear, coming from behind. She blinked and couldn't believe her eyes. The snake had gone, frightened by a long spear now sticking out of the ground.

A shadow fell over her and she turned, giving another gasp of fear at the sight of the tall young Maasai warrior standing over her. But she fell back with a sigh of relief as she recognised the man as the Maasai with the sick wife for whom Morgan had brought medicine. 'Oh, thank you! Thank you!'

The young warrior bowed his head respectfully, then walked over to pull out the spear. He said something to Lexi, pointing a long thin finger at various parts of her body.

She gave him a tremulous smile. 'If you're asking me if I'm injured, I don't think anything is broken, but I'm going to feel these bruises for a long time.'

The young man said something else, looking about him, and she heard the name, 'Morgan.'

She struggled to get to her feet, but only managed a sitting position. 'Oh, dear . . . I think I'm going to need some help here . . . ' She had struggled to her knees while talking, then held out her hand, which they young Maasai stared at for a moment, then he smiled, nodded and came forward.

'*Pole-pole!*' he said, showing her the palms of his hands in a sign that obviously meant that she should take her time.

'That's it! *Pole-pole!* That's what Matthew told me to say to Mbaya! It's nothing like 'haraka' is it?'

'*Haraka! Hapana, bi! Pole-pole! Pole-pole!*' The Maasai took her hands and pulled her slowly to her feet. She stood, swaying on legs that didn't seem to belong to her. The Maasai stepped back and beckoned to her. She took a faltering step forward and winced as every muscle and joint in her body cried out for mercy.

'Redlands?' she asked him, hoping he would understand. 'Which way? How do I get back there?'

The Maasai patted his chest, pointed

into the distance, then smiled and offered her his hand again. With his help she struggled up from the hollow on to flat ground. In the distance she could make out the tall acacia trees that surrounded Redlands.

It was a long and agonising walk, but the Maasai stayed with her every step of the way, giving her encouragement, speaking to her softly all the while in Swahili. Every now and then the name Morgan was clearly recognisable and it was spoken with such reverence that there was no doubt he was held in high esteem by this man.

As the white gateposts of Redlands came into view a safari jeep came out and pulled up a few feet in front of them. Morgan got out and raised a hand in greeting to the Maasai. '*Jambo, Mbatian!*' Then he turned his gaze to Lexi and, reaching out, held her firmly, his hands gripping her arms. 'Little fool! What were you thinking of, riding Mbaya? Christine says you wouldn't listen to her . . . just took off . . . '

'I didn't. Christine told me . . . oh, it doesn't matter.'

He looked at her, at the bruises, the scratches and the torn shirt, and his grip relaxed.

'Are you all right?' he asked in a more gentle tone and suddenly she wanted to cry, but she bit her lip and nodded, blinking back the tears that threatened to flow.

Morgan turned to Mbatian, thanking him. The men shook hands, and then the young Maasai nodded to Lexi, smiling shyly.

'Thank you,' she said, then turned to Morgan, 'he saved my life. Thank you seems so inadequate and I can't even say it in his language!'

'Say *asante sana*. He'll understand.'

'*Asante sana, Mbatian*,' Lexi was acutely aware that Morgan had an arm around her and she was leaning heavily against him.

Mbatian raised a hand, smiled again, turned and walked away.

'Let's get back home,' Morgan said.

'I'm going to call the doctor and have him check you over. Can you walk or should I carry you?'

'I'm perfectly all right!' Lexi said, not feeling all right at all, but not wishing to appear weak. 'Shouldn't you be looking for Mbaya? She dashed off somewhere in that direction.'

'Mbaya's fine. She came home by herself. That's why I knew something was wrong. I was worried about you . . . '

He swung her round to face him and held her close, looking down searchingly into her face. She felt the weakness from her fall increase, or was it because of his closeness? Her knees gave way and she slumped against him, her head on his broad chest. His heart thudded rapidly against her ear.

'You're causing me all sort of problems, you know, Lexi,' he said softly. 'You've no idea how difficult it is . . . ' His words tailed off and she felt his hand stroking her hair in one slow, deliberate movement. She remembered what Christine had said about him attracting women, what he himself had said about the young women who foolishly threw themselves at wealthy men.

She pulled back from him. 'I'm sorry I'm a bother. I think the sooner I go back to England, the better.'

# Morgan Makes A Move

'Miss Merrill?' Lexi looked up as the unexpected voice interrupted her thoughts. Maria, the Tyler's maid, was hovering shyly in the doorway.

'Yes, Maria?'

'You okay, Miss Merrill? I go now for my night off?'

'Yes, of course. Don't worry about me, Maria. I'm fine.'

'Matthew say you were in an accident! That horse, Mbaya, only Mister Morgan understand her. Everybody know that! Why then you ride her?'

'Because I'm all kinds of a fool, Maria.' Lexi shifted her position on the lounger and winced.

'Mister Morgan, he very angry! He shout and wave his arms about like crazy man.'

'I'm afraid I have an unhappy knack

of making Mister Morgan angry,' Lexi sighed and was surprised to see the maid shake her head vehemently.

'Oh, no, Miss Merrill! He not angry at you! He angry at Miss Christine! He say she wicked for doing bad thing to you. He send her away. I never see Mister Morgan so angry. He usually very nice. Everybody like him. You ask my William.'

'William?' Lexi remembered the big African who was the Tyler's driver and guide.

'Yes. William is my man. We get married soon. Now, you be all right? You need anything?'

'No, really, I'm fine. Goodnight, Maria.'

The girl smiled broadly and bowed her head before turning and hurrying down the hallway.

★   ★   ★

Lexi lay back against the cushions and stared out at the black, velvety evening, diamond-studded with shimmering stars. Through the silence, the jungle sounds crept in; the roar of a lion, the trumpeting of an elephant, the warning call of a bird, the chirruping of insects.

Lexi couldn't remember ever feeling so alone, and yet she didn't feel lonely. Somehow, she thought, it was impossible to feel lonely in a country so teeming with life. Kenya was beautiful. It was exciting. It could so easily be her kind of country, if only things had been different.

She closed her eyes and tried to be more positive, but her brain refused to get rid of the memories of the past few days.

\* \* \*

Having got back to the house, she had spent a long time soaking in a hot bath, trying to soothe away the aches and pains of her fall. Christine had been nowhere to be seen. The doctor had arrived and checked her all over, happily pronouncing her intact and a 'very lucky young woman.'

Belle, of course, had been furious about the whole affair and promised to give Christine a piece of her mind when they met later that evening. Apparently, there was to be a party over at the Benson house, a celebration in honour of Christine's twenty-first birthday.

The entire Tyler family were going to the celebrations. Belle was full of apologies for leaving Lexi on her own, but Lexi didn't mind at all. She had persuaded Bobbie to wear one of her chic cocktail dresses. The dress fitted the girl a treat, its plain and simple lines flattering her youthful figure. With a little help from Lexi, Bobbie went to the party looking like a radiant Cinderella.

Lexi hadn't seen Morgan since afternoon tea, when he had politely enquired after her wellbeing. On being assured that she was fine, he simply nodded and left her. His face had been set resolutely, his eyes guarded, giving nothing away.

Lexi stirred as she recalled that brief moment when he had held her close. Had he been going to kiss her? How she wished now that she had not been so foolish as to pull away from him. What harm would there have been in a kiss, a small, intimate memory of Morgan Tyler to take with her back to England. And to remember for the rest of her life.

'So this is where you are!'

Lexi opened her eyes and felt flames of embarrassment rush to her cheeks. She had no idea how long Morgan had been standing there looking at her, but here he was, looking resplendent in a white jacket, bow tie and black trousers.

'I'm sorry?' she faltered, swinging her feet to the floor and suppressing a grimace as her stiff joints complained bitterly.

'I was expecting you to be at the party.' Morgan fixed her with a questioning stare, one eyebrow characteristically raised. 'Belle said you weren't coming. Why is that? Are you more shaken up than you care to admit?'

'I can't say that I feel exactly wonderful at this precise moment.' Lexi wanted to look away but found that she couldn't; she was hypnotised by those cool, grey eyes.

'That's not the reason, though, is it?'

'No, it isn't.'

'The reason wouldn't have anything to do with me, would it?'

What was he doing? Was this some kind of trap he was laying to prove that she was the type of woman he suspected her of being? Well, she wasn't going to take the bait.

'Why should it have anything to do with you?' she said coolly. 'I wasn't exactly invited and I make a point of never going anywhere where I'm not wanted.'

'Is that so? Well, young woman, let me tell you that you *have* been invited, and if you're not ready in thirty minutes, you can come with me just the way you are.'

130

'I'm the last person Christine would want to see at her birthday party.'

'I don't care what that silly child wants. *I* want you to be there.'

'And do you always get what you want?'

'When I want it badly enough. Now, go upstairs and get changed into something stunning . . . and something which shows your bruises. I want Christine to be so full of remorse she'll never attempt anything as crazy as that again.'

'Is that the only reason you want me there, to humiliate Christine?'

Morgan flashed her a look of impatience, then, walking over to her, gripped her wrists and pulled her none too gently to her feet. She gasped as her muscles strained painfully beneath the bruises caused by her tumble.

'No, Lexi, it isn't the reason,' he said in a low voice and moved back a strand of her hair with one finger.

Lexi was suddenly finding it difficult to swallow and her heart fluttered inside her chest like a trapped butterfly.

'It may take me a little more than half an hour,' she said, and made to move away from Morgan, but he stopped her, his hands resting gently on her shoulders.

'It was a kind thing you did for Bobbie this evening,' he said and smiled one of his rare smiles that warmed his eyes and sent a shiver through Lexi. 'Thank you. It meant a lot to her . . . and to me.'

'I like Bobbie.'

'She likes you, too.'

'I'm glad someone here does!'

'Go on . . . get changed.' He hesitated, then: 'Lexi . . . ?'

'Yes?'

'Take as long as you want. I'll wait.'

★ ★ ★

Lexi took exactly thirty-five minutes from leaving the terrace to reappearing in a light blue strapless dress. She had obviously chosen well, since Morgan gave her an appraising look that told her he was impressed.

'That colour suits you!' he commented, as he held out his hand. 'Shall we go?'

When they got outside, Lexi was glad to see they were to travel by shiny black Audi rather than by open Jeep. And when Morgan handed her into the passenger seat, she was very much aware of his hand beneath her elbow, his fingers gentle and cool on her skin.

★   ★   ★

It was no more than a fifteen minute drive to the Bensons. They lived in an old colonial manor house in Nairobi. The long, winding drive up to the portico entrance with its white marble columns and hanging baskets of scarlet geraniums, was lit by old British gas lamp posts which had been converted to electricity.

A white liveried servant ran out to greet them as they rode up. Morgan got out and threw the man his car keys.

'Good evening, George! How is that new son of yours?'

'Evenin' Mister Morgan! Good to see you, sir! Young Tyler Morgan is doing just fine, thank you very much!'

Morgan stepped around the car and opened the door at Lexi's side, holding out his hand to her, which she took gratefully.

'He called his son after you?' she said to Morgan.

'I'm afraid so.' Morgan's face creased into a genuinely humourous grin. 'I suppose we have to be glad his wife didn't produce a girl. They were determined that whatever the gender, the next of their offspring was going to bear my name!'

'What did you do to deserve that?'

'Oh, not very much, really. Sometimes the Africans take gratitude a bit too far . . . ' He winced as George drove his car off with an agonising scream of tyres and a crunching of the gears. 'I must find time to give George some driving lessons! Let's go in, shall we . . . and Lexi . . . '

'Yes?'

He had turned her to face him, hands placed on both shoulders. With difficulty she kept an indifferent expression on her face, glad that he could not possibly know the turmoil he had put her emotions into just by touching her.

'You look very beautiful this evening . . . '

Her knees began to turn to water.

'Thank you, Morgan . . . ' she murmured.

'But I guess you're going through agony with those bruises, so if this evening becomes too much for you, don't be afraid to say and I'll take you back home.'

A sudden wave of irritation swept aside all other emotions. Lexi gritted her teeth. Did he have to spoil the compliment by acting as though she was a child?

'I'm not as fragile as you seem to think,' she said. 'I'm a Merrill. When we fall, we bounce right back!'

Morgan looked at her, wide surprise in his eyes, then his head went back and he let out a loud guffaw of laughter before escorting her up the steps and into the sumptuous Benson household.

★ ★ ★

It was almost as if a pre-arranged signal had passed through the house, for women of all ages suddenly flocked to pay homage to Morgan Tyler. It was embarrassing, Lexi thought, the way they danced attendance on the man. And, of course, Morgan lapped it up. No-one was left out or ignored. He spoke to them all, seemed to know them and their families intimately.

Mr and Mrs Benson came over and greeted him warmly, eyeing Lexi with ill-concealed surprise. It was obvious they had not expected her to be here.

'There you are, Morgan! What on earth kept you . . . ?' Christine Benson's voice tailed off. 'Oh . . . hello, Lexi!'

'Hello, Christine.' Lexi smiled, but was unable to impart any warmth toward her young hostess. 'Happy birthday. Thank you for inviting me.'

'Well . . . I . . . er . . . ' Christine looked about her uncomfortably; people were sensing an atmosphere between the two young women, one a stranger with visible bruises. Music struck up in the next room as a small band played an up-tempo number. Couples drifted off and began dancing. Christine grabbed Morgan's hand. 'Come on, Morgan!'

'Sorry, Christine.' Morgan pulled back and put an arm around Lexi's waist. 'This is Lexi's dance.'

'Oh, but . . . !' The corners of Christine's mouth drooped and she became the picture of a spoilt child.

'You don't have to dance with me just because you brought me,' Lexi said, as Morgan led her on to the crowded floor.

'I don't *have* to do anything.'

He spoke the words close to her ear, his breath ruffling her.

'I want to dance with you. Is that such a crime?'

'Of course not. I just . . . ' Her voice caught in her throat as he took her in his arms and held her closer than she thought was necessary.

Lexi lifted her head and looked up into his face, surprised to see him smiling down at her, and she smiled back. Maybe it was going to be a lovely evening, after all.

★   ★   ★

It was surprising how Lexi forgot her aches and pains, especially when she was dancing in Morgan's strong arms. He didn't dance every dance with her, but there was no shortage of partners, all of whom seemed to compete for her favours, wanting to know the details of her accident.

'I made the mistake of riding Morgan's horse and listening to the wrong advice,' Lexi told anyone who asked.

'No-one, but no-one, rides Morgan Tyler's horse!' one young man announced as he whirled her around the floor.

'Well, I did.' she laughed, 'and I have the bruises to prove it.'

'I thought everybody in Kenya knew about Mbaya. You must be pretty new in town,' the young man went on.

'You could say that.'

'So, when are you going to name the day?'

'I beg your pardon?'

'You and Morgan! I presume you are going to make an honest man of him? It's about time someone did.'

'Oh! Oh, no . . . I mean . . . we . . . we're just . . . well, just friends.'

'Come off it! Who are you trying to fool? We've all noticed the way he looks at you.'

Lexi flushed and quickly changed the subject by talking about the air controllers' strike, only to be informed that it was all but over. 'Over? Are you sure?'

'Yes, of course. Everything will be

back to normal by the weekend.'

'How do you know?'

'Because I'm one of them,' her dancing partner told her. 'All being well, we'll be back at work on Saturday morning.'

'I see.' Lexi felt a great sinking feeling as she realised her visit to Kenya was almost over. She would never again see Morgan Tyler; never melt beneath the gaze of those hypnotic eyes. His hands would never touch her, nor his lips kiss her, nor his deep voice charm her. She would never know what it was like to be loved by him.

★ ★ ★

She was standing talking to Belle when they struck up the strains of the last waltz. The older woman looked up sharply, a shadow of consternation passing across her face.

'Oh, Lord! Lexi, ever since my husband died I haven't been able to cope with the last waltz. I'm off. Tell

Rusty I've taken the car. He and Bobbie can come home with you and Morgan, can't they?'

Belle reached out and squeezed Lexi's arm, then she was gone in a swirl of brilliant silk kaftan.

★   ★   ★

Lexi understood what Belle must be feeling right now. The last waltz was always the most important dance of the evening, to be saved for husband and wife, and lovers old and new. She looked around her and saw Morgan on the other side of the room. Their eyes met briefly, then he broke away from the elderly couple he was talking to and started to move in her direction. She held her breath, then let it out slowly and painfully as she saw Christine sally forth and throw herself into Morgan's arms, drawing him on to the dance floor. She saw Morgan's look of annoyance and his feeble attempt to extricate himself, but then became resigned to his fate. To object too strongly would cause an ugly scene and Lexi felt sure that it wasn't in Morgan's nature to do such a thing.

\* \* \*

'Hi!'

Lexi turned around.

'Hello, Rusty.' She smiled, hoping he would not ask her to dance, relieved when he didn't. 'Where's Bobbie? You two seem to be having a grand time.'

'Oh, she's around somewhere. The silly kid got upset about something or other and ran off. I think it was my fault, in a way, but for the life of me I don't know why.'

'I'm sorry about that. I had hoped she would enjoy this evening. She was looking so pretty!'

'Yeah. Amazing, really. I hear it was all your doing?'

'It didn't take much.'

'Well, it was pretty good of you. Most

people didn't recognise her, she looked so fabulous!'

'I hope you told her how good she looked.'

'She wouldn't have taken any notice of me. I'm just like a brother to her.'

'Have you ever thought of being more than a brother, Rusty? She likes you an awful lot, you know.'

Rusty turned back to the couples gliding across the floor. His mournful eyes followed Morgan and Christine.

'Liking somebody an awful lot isn't enough,' he said in a low, detached voice as if speaking to himself. 'They have to like you back.'

Lexi's eyes narrowed as the truth behind his revealing statement became clear. Poor Rusty. He was in love with Christine. And Christine was in love with Morgan. And Bobbie was in love with Rusty. And she, Lexi, who was loved by nobody in particular, was trying desperately not to fall in love with a man she could never have. What a crazy mix-up of emotions.

The music faded and the dancers drifted off the floor. People were collecting coats and wraps and getting into cars and saying goodnight and what a wonderful party it had been. Morgan was dragged, protesting, by an insistent Christine through a door at the far end of the room, which was firmly closed behind them. When they reappeared some fifteen minutes later, Christine looked flushed, Morgan looked slightly less than composed and there was lipstick on his cheek and his collar that was a perfect match to the glistening pink on Christine's lips.

'But you can't possibly want to go home yet!' Christine was saying in a too loud voice, making sure that anyone who was left could hear. 'I mean, I haven't finished thanking you for my gorgeous birthday present. Oh, Morgan, darling, it's so beautiful!'

She was fingering an emerald and diamond leaf brooch set in gold, which was pinned to her white silk gown.

'I've had enough for one night, young lady,' Morgan was saying as they joined Rusty and Lexi, who were ready to go. 'Besides, I don't think you deserve such a gift. Not after what you did to Lexi. By the way, have you apologised for that brainless stunt yet?'

Christine pouted and gave an indignant sigh, then looked directly at Lexi.

'I apologise,' she said flatly. 'Of course, if you hadn't assured me that you could ride I would never have done it. It was supposed to be a joke.'

'It was a childish trick and extremely dangerous,' Morgan said. 'I hope I never find you trying anything like that again.'

Christine tried to look sheepish as she gazed up at Morgan. He simply shook his head, then bent and placed a light kiss on her cheek. 'Goodnight, Christine. Well, folks, are we ready? Where are Belle and Bobbie?'

'Belle went home a little while ago,' Lexi informed him, trying not to look at the smudge of lipstick on his cheek. 'I don't know where Bobbie is.'

'I'm here!'

Bobbie was hovering in the shadows behind them. She moved forward a step, but was reluctant to come any further. Lexi saw at once that the girl had been crying. She went to her and put an arm about her shoulders. 'Come on, Bobbie,' she said, as cheerfully as she could manage. 'Let's wait for the men outside. I could do with a breath of air.'

★ ★ ★

The atmosphere was heavy during the journey home. All four seemed to be preoccupied with their own private thoughts. Bobbie sniffed and rubbed surreptitiously at her damp eyes, smudging what little was left of the mascara she had applied under Lexi's direction. Rusty stared sulkily out into the black night and looked as if he wished it would swallow him up. As for

Morgan, he seemed to have difficulty concentrating on his driving and fumbled with the gears on at least two occasions.

Once, Lexi looked up to see his eyes framed in the driving mirror. He was staring at her in that characteristically disconcerting manner he had. She held his gaze for as long as she could, then dragged her eyes away and out into the dark night.

'Well, I've had it,' Rusty mumbled sleepily as they all got out of the car at Redlands. 'Goodnight.'

'Rusty . . . I . . . can I get you some warm milk?' Bobbie trotted behind him hopefully. 'I'm going to have some.'

'Enjoy it, funny face! See you tomorrow.'

Morgan's face was tight as he watched them disappear down the hall.

'Poor kid!' he sighed. 'She never gives up and he's too engrossed in himself to notice her.'

'You know about Bobbie, about the way she feels about Rusty?' Lexi had turned, poised on the second stair on the way up to her room. It put her at eye-level with Morgan, who looked even more devastatingly handsome in the golden glow from the hall light.

'Yes, of course I know.' He sighed and shook his head. 'It's a funny old world, isn't it. Everybody wasting their lives chasing impossible dreams. We all ought to have better sense and just settle for what comes along. After all, that pot of gold at the end of the rainbow dissolves into harsh reality as soon as we reach out and try to touch it.'

'And which pot of gold are you chasing, Morgan?' Lexi asked, keeping her voice light and casual, although she was suddenly aware of a fluttering in her chest as he came nearer to her, his hand on the banister almost touching hers.

'I've done my chasing,' he said, coming even closer, so that her heart beat faster and her throat became dry. 'I'm now debating whether or not I should just reach out and take what I want.'

Lexi felt him draw her slowly towards him. Two hearts quickened simultaneously and beat almost as one.

'Morgan . . . I . . . I don't . . . '

One of his hands was pressing against the small of her back; the other had reached up and was caressing her hair, her cheek, her ear, her mouth.

'I really don't think . . . '

'Do shut up, Lexi,' Morgan whispered, and she felt his lips gently meet hers.

Her senses reeling, she slid her arms about his neck, not caring about the consequences. Morgan pulled his head back and groaned, 'Lexi!' He seemed to throw the word up at the high ceiling; it echoed in her ear as if they were in some hollow chamber floating giddily in space. 'I can't remember the last time this happened to me.'

Lexi felt something stab her heart as she remembered the reputation Morgan had. Remembered how he himself had treated her not so very long ago. And there was that trace of Christine's lipstick on his cheek. What an idiot she was.

She pushed him away from her, her hands against his chest.

'Stop it, Morgan! What do you think I am? A pot of gold for the taking? Let me tell you, you've got me all wrong. I'm not one of your adoring women. I suggest you go and find one of them. I gather you have plenty!'

He released her and stepped back. There was a momentary expression of hurt in those smouldering eyes, then it was gone and his jaws clamped shut in anger.

'I don't know where you get your facts,' he said coldly, 'but I suggest you question your source.'

'I have no reason to worry about it one way or the other. In a very short time I'll be leaving and our paths will never cross again. Perhaps you thought I would welcome a brief encounter with someone I would never see again. Well, that may be your way, but it's certainly not mine.'

'Lexi ... ' He reached out and grabbed her wrist, but she wrenched it away and ran stumbling up the stairs away from him.

# A Magical Trip

'How are you getting on at Secretarial College, Bobbie?' Lexi asked, needing to break the tense silence that reigned over the breakfast table the following morning.

Bobbie looked up from her toast and marmalade and gave a wry smile as she licked a sticky finger. Gone was the blossoming new womanhood of last night. Back was Bobbie the plain-faced tomboy with the troubled eyes.

'It's all right, I suppose,' she said, before throwing her napkin down and getting to her feet. 'I don't think I'll ever be as good as Maggie, though.'

'Really? Who's Maggie?'

But Bobbie was already leaving the patio at a run, probably because she didn't want to face Rusty, who was just arriving.

'Who's Maggie?' Lexi asked again

and glanced furtively at Morgan beneath her long lashes; but either he didn't hear her or he was just going to ignore her for the rest of her short stay at Redlands. His head was down and he was making a great production number of buttering his toast.

'Maggie is our secretary, Lexi, although she hasn't been in for a few days. Some kind of tummy bug, I believe,' Belle said.

'She's an excellent secretary,' Morgan said.

Belle laughed and poured herself a large glass of fresh orange. 'She's one of Morgan's lame ducks, Lexi,' she explained. 'Though I'd hate the poor girl to hear me say that. Now, Morgan, don't look at me like that. You know yourself, she wouldn't have a job if it hadn't been for you taking her on when nobody else would. And before you blow me up for saying that, I have to agree she turned out to be a pretty good investment. In fact, if she doesn't come back to work soon we shall be in trouble.'

'I shouldn't think the great Morgan Tyler would have any difficulty enlisting the services of another secretary!' Rusty said, as he rose from the table, his breakfast untouched.

'Oh, good grief! When will you two stop sparring and behave like grown men!' Belle shook her head. 'Will you excuse me, Lexi? I have a long list of phone calls to make and a host of letters to write, which I positively hate to do, but needs must.'

'Can I help?' Lexi was anxious not to be left alone with Morgan, who was showing no sign of leaving the table.

Belle hesitated, then a slow smile spread over her face. 'Of course! You're a secretary, aren't you? What a marvellous idea!'

Lexi felt Morgan's eyes on her. She met them and swallowed hard, remembering last night and his lips on hers . . . and she had pushed him away.

'There won't be time for that, I'm afraid, Belle.' He was still staring at

Lexi as he spoke, his eyes both challenging and accusing.

'Why not, dear? Oh, don't say the strike is over?'

'No, but it will be soon and I want Lexi to take more than just a memory of Redlands home with her. I have to fly up to Keekorok. There's an elderly couple up there whose guide is ill. They're old and loyal clients. I said I'd take them around for a couple of days' safari. You did say you wanted to see some of the wild life, didn't you, Lexi?'

'Well, yes, but . . . '

'So pack a few things. We'll be leaving in an hour.'

'I . . . I think perhaps I'd be better employed helping Belle.'

'No you won't, my dear!' Belle patted her hand. 'You'll do exactly as the big boss man here tells you to. Lexi, you'd never forgive yourself if you threw up a chance to see the Masai Mara. Why, it's one of the greatest game reserves in the whole of Africa, if not the world. And Morgan, here, is a superb guide. No, you go with Morgan. I insist!'

She drifted off and they could hear her sandals slapping the dark oak flooring down the hall.

'You didn't have to suggest that I go with you,' Lexi said evenly. 'Look, Morgan, rather than cause any more unpleasantness, I think it would be best if you simply took me into Nairobi. Surely I could find a hotel room somewhere.'

'Lexi . . . ' Morgan said, 'about last night . . . I apologise for my behaviour. I'd had a heck of a day, what with one thing and another, and you . . . '

'I was available, or so you mistakenly thought!'

'Lexi, I know you probably won't believe me, but you're the first woman I've kissed like that since my wife walked out on me.'

'Please . . . I don't want to talk about it.'

Morgan straightened up and said coolly, 'Very well. If that's what you want.'

'That's what I want.'

'In that case, can we call a truce for as long as you are here? I really would like to show you the Mara. And don't worry. We won't be alone, if that's what's bothering you. William is coming with us. I also promised Christine that she could come.'

'Christine!'

'I know how you feel about her.' Morgan gave a lop-sided excuse for a smile, 'but she's been going through a tough time recently. You know, being rich and spoiled isn't a pre-requisite for happiness. In many ways, Christine is one of the unhappiest people I've ever met.'

'She's unhappy because she wants you and you're the first thing she's ever been denied!' Lexi said, her anger rising as she thought of Christine. Then she remembered the lipstick. 'Or has she?'

'You really are determined to turn me into some kind of womaniser, aren't you, Lexi? As for my relationship with Christine, perhaps a lesser man would be tempted, but not me. Definitely not me. I'd like you to believe that.'

Lexi ran trembling fingers through her hair and avoided his eyes so that he would not know he had the power to turn her to a quivering mass of jelly. 'I suppose I'd better pack a bag,' she said.

'Not too much and everything casual and comfortable.' She sensed a faint hint of relief in his words, as if he'd been worried she would refuse to go with him.

★   ★   ★

As the small aircraft with Morgan at the controls circled over the vast planes of the Masai Mara, Lexi strained forward, peering down at the flat red and yellow ochre landscape with its teeming wildlife. She felt like a child pressed against a shop window at Christmas.

'Wildebeest!' William pointed out a long procession of dark, grey-brown gnu, large heads bobbing as they walked, one behind the other, across the shimmering savannah.

'Hundreds of them!' Lexi cried in amazement.

'Thousands! They go on annual migration, following the food and water.' William's broad muscular arm shot out. 'Look! Look there!'

Lexi followed the line of his pointing finger and gave an exclamation of delight. Just below them and to the left a herd of long necked giraffes were grazing, reaching up to feed from the high branches of a large acacia tree. As they moved off, their movements were beautiful, liquid slow-motion to those watching from above.

'This is incredible!' Lexi exclaimed delightedly as William again pointed, this time to where a herd of brightly striped zebra drank at a water hole.

'You like my country, Miss Merrill?' William said.

'Oh, yes, William! I think it's the most exciting, beautiful place on earth!'

'I'm glad. I am very proud of my heritage. Some people would like to change it. I will fight to keep it the way it is.'

There was a loud sigh from the seat opposite and Christine threw down the magazine she was reading. 'William, do shut up! You're so boring. This country is boring. The sooner it changes, the better. I mean, who needs all this empty space with nothing but silly animals to look at.'

'You should not talk like this, Miss Benson. It is bad talk.'

'Oh, it's great for the tourists, I grant you, but who would want to live here? Believe me, William, there's only one thing keeping me here, and we all know what that is, don't we?' Christine shot a knowing smile in Lexi's direction, then got out of her seat and made her way forward to the cockpit, where she slipped into the co-pilot's seat next to Morgan.

William muttered a few angry words in Swahili and shook his head. 'I am sorry, Miss Merrill, but that girl makes me say bad things. I do not wish to offend you.'

'I'm not offended, William.' Lexi smiled and tried to take her attention away from the beautiful girl who was doing her best to distract the pilot.

★　★　★

Keekorok Lodge, like many of the other safari centres, was suffering from a lack of clientele because of the air controllers' strike. The place seemed strangely quiet and deserted.

Morgan deposited Lexi and Christine in the terraced lounge with iced tropical fruit drinks and went off in search of the two elderly clients who had specifically requested him as their guide.

William had met some friends and was doing some socialising with many friendly slaps on the back and jovial laughter.

'Well, this is very nice, isn't it?' Lexi took a long, grateful sip of her drink and looked around her. She felt the need to try to be sociable towards

Christine, despite the girl's hostile nature. 'Do you know this place well?'

'Of course I do! Morgan has brought me up here many times.'

'You're very lucky to have a place like this to visit.'

'I hate this place! It's boring. The people who come here are boring.'

'Then why do you come?'

'Need you ask?' Their eyes met and there was no need for further explanation. Christine came because of Morgan. 'Now, you, Lexi, are a different kettle of fish. I can't make you out at all. I mean, having made a fool of yourself over Rusty, why on earth are you still hanging around? Don't you find it all just too humiliating?'

'A little, yes.' Lexi lay back in the cushions of her wicker chair and tried to relax. 'But I don't have much choice. I wanted to find a hotel somewhere until the strike was over, but Morgan insisted that I stay at Redlands.'

'And why would he do that? After all, he doesn't think much of gold-diggers, especially when they're after his gold.'

Lexi bit her lip and held on tightly to her composure. 'I'm no gold-digger, Christine. Rusty just happened to come along when I was feeling particularly vulnerable. I think it may have been the same for him. Fortunately, we realised our mistake before it was too late. End of story.'

'Rusty would have gone through with it,' Christine smirked and ran a red-painted finger-nail around the lip of her glass. 'It was Morgan who put an end to your silly affair. Rusty would still marry you, if you gave him half a chance.'

'It wouldn't be right for either of us.'

'You'd do worse than to marry him, you know.'

'I'm not in love with Rusty any more than he's in love with me,' Lexi said with certainty.

'Well, there's no-one else around that's free, so you'd better head back home.'

Before Lexi could respond to this,

Morgan reappeared. He approached the two young women with a dark, thoughtful frown on his handsome face. His broad shoulders were slightly slumped and his hands were thrust deep into his pockets.

'What is it?' Lexi asked, as he sat down next to her.

'The Bromleys . . . the old couple we were supposed to join up with here . . . they've had to go back to Nairobi.' He lay back, sinking against the cushioned chairback. 'The husband had a heart attack, would you believe. They had to fly him out as an emergency. Unfortunately, no-one thought to contact me.'

'The poor man! Is it serious?'

'Difficult to tell. He was over seventy, apparently. Not very fit, but determined to see Africa before he died.'

'Silly old fool!' Christine exclaimed disdainfully.

'That's not very charitable, is it, Christine?' Morgan said. He waved over a waiter and ordered tea and sandwiches for the three of them.

'So what do we do now?' Lexi ventured. 'Fly back to Redlands?'

Morgan shook his head. 'No, I said I'd show you the Mara and that's what I'm going to do. I've booked us in here for a couple of days. In many ways, I welcome the break. I'm in need of some relaxation. I haven't had much in the last few years, what with one thing and another.'

'You really don't have to do this just for me, you know.' Lexi felt embarrassed. 'I mean, I realise my being here has put you all in a difficult situation . . . '

'Lexi,' Morgan said, 'if you knew me at all, you would know that I never do anything unless I want to.'

'Oh, well, in that case thank you. I'm grateful. It's just . . . well, I feel so guilty about what's happened . . . Rusty and me, I mean . . . '

'Forget it . . . ' He reached over and gave her hand a squeeze that made her heart trip, and made Christine sit up and take notice, a flash of jealousy souring her expression. 'Let's see if we can be friends, at least for the next forty-eight hours.'

'All right,' she nodded and gave him a blushing smile, aware that his hand was lingering on hers and his eyes were searching her face almost as if they were seeing her for the first time and liking what they saw.

It would be so easy to fall under his spell, Lexi thought. But she was determined she wasn't going to be just another silly woman on his long list of adoring conquests.

'Has there been any word about the strike being over?' she asked, pulling her hand away.

It was Christine who answered. 'They were due back at noon today, according to the radio. Do you mean to say you didn't know, Lexi?'

'No, I didn't!' Lexi looked from Christine back to Morgan, who averted his gaze for a second before responding. 'There was some mention of it, but . . . ' He shrugged and gave his lopsided smile that made him look so youthful. 'Well, anyway, I'm sure you would rather spend another two days here seeing the wildlife, Lexi. Besides, it'll take a few days to get things back to normal. I doubt whether you'd be able to get booked on any of the first flights out.'

'It looks like you weren't going to give me the choice.' Lexi smiled back at him despite herself and was aware of Christine's scathing look.

'Well, at least you'll have some worthwhile memories to take back home with you.' Morgan smiled again and the warmth reached his eyes; it was like seeing the sun coming out from behind a cloud and it had a most disarming affect on Lexi.

★ ★ ★

Lunch was enjoyable, despite Christine's brooding silence. Afterwards, Morgan took them to their individual cabins. Lexi was relieved to find she didn't have to share with the younger girl.

She spent all of five minutes unpacking her few belongings and then went out to explore the vast grounds of Keekorok, having promised Morgan that she would meet him in an hour at the main reception area so he could take her out on her first safari.

Outside her cabin, a large acacia tree housed eight malibou storks sitting in its uppermost branches. As she stared up at them, shading her eyes from the hot, blinding sun, more birds flew in, balancing with amazing agility, apparently unperturbed by the long, needle-like thorns.

Around her feet, bright iridescent small birds hopped about the dry, sandy earth. Their unexpected beauty made her catch her breath and exclaim her delight audibly. There was every colour imaginable from bright yellow through every shade of blue, and there was one light grey bird, bigger than the rest, with a huge red painted bill.

She had been standing some time openly admiring the birds when a soft chuckle from behind startled her and she turned to find William watching her.

He grinned broadly. 'You are like a little girl looking at pretty gems,' he said.

'Oh dear, William. Am I that bad?'

'Not bad! Good. These pretty little birds make you happy. With some, it takes a lot more than pretty little birds.'

'But they're so beautiful! I've never seen anything like them. What are they, William?'

He pointed the birds out for her, proud to impart his knowledge. 'The bright blue ones with the orange breast and the white ring, they are starlings.'

'Starlings! But they're nothing like our starlings at home!'

'The yellow birds are weavers,' William continued, 'and the big one there with the red bill . . . that's a red-billed hornbill. See, take this piece of bread. Hold it on your hand, close to

169

the ground, and keep very still. They will feed from your hand.'

Lexi took the crust of bread he offered, broke a few small pieces off and did as he had instructed. After a minute or two she was delighted to find one or two birds bravely coming forward for the bread. The final piece she offered to the hornbill which, despite his size, was more reticent. However, after a few minutes of gentle coaxing, the bird edged forward and took the bread from her fingers. She was amazed at the gentleness of the action from such a fierce looking bill.

'Oh, how marvellous!'

William laughed, a deep, rumbling chortle, then he stiffened visibly and fell silent as Christine swung haughtily past them dressed in a bikini and making for the camp's pool.

'Enjoy your swim, Christine,' Lexi said in a friendly voice.

'I will, believe me. Why don't you join me? Or is your swimming like your riding?'

Lexi ignored the pointed remark. 'There's far too much to see here,' she said. 'I don't want to waste my time in the pool.'

'Good! In that case, I'll have Morgan to myself. I've told him to meet me there. See you later, then.'

'Yes. See you later.'

'That one is big trouble, Miss Merrill,' William said.

'I think it's Morgan you should be telling that to, William,' Lexi said, and then touched his arm gently. 'I'm sorry. It's really none of my business.'

'Morgan knows all about Miss Christine. He knows things have gone too far and must be stopped. Believe me, Miss Merrill, he will do something soon. You will see. When she was young, he was like her big brother. He used to laugh at her funny little ways. But now, she is no longer a child.'

'I think we are all aware of that, William!'

'Morgan is too kind,' William said. 'That is always his problem. He doesn't like to hurt people. But you will see. He has it all worked out about Miss Christine.'

'I wish I had your confidence in him.' Lexi smiled ruefully and William frowned, but said nothing. 'Anyway, I'll soon be back home in England, and all this . . . Kenya, Rusty, Morgan, Christine . . . will be no more than a fading memory.'

'No, Miss Merrill! No! You will stay.'

'No, William, you're wrong . . . Oh, so wrong. And the name's Lexi.'

'Here . . . ' William thrust a well-worn bird identification book into her hands. 'You take this. It will help you to learn the birds.'

'Oh, thank you, William! Can I hang on to it until . . . until I leave?'

'You will not leave, I say!'

Lexi sighed. 'Thanks for the book, William.'

'You are welcome, Miss . . . Lexi. And don't forget, we meet at two for the safari.'

★ ★ ★

Lexi walked down a grassy slope away from the camp buildings and found a tree-shrouded wooden walkway lined with old fashioned lanterns. It wasn't much cooler here beneath the trees, but at least they shaded her from the scorching sun. She followed the walkway until it came out into a large observation hide. In the centre was a small bar. The young barman grinned a welcome as she entered.

'*Jambo, bi!*' he said, as he poured a bucketful of ice into a container and set up bottles of orange juice and beer on the counter.

'*Jambo!*' Lexi replied, pleased to have learned at least one word of Swahili.

'You like drink?'

'No, thank you.' She shook her head and walked to the far rail. The sight that met her eyes was breathtaking. Beneath the lookout was a large waterhole and as she watched, wildebeest wandered in to drink. A few minutes later, a group of black and white striped zebras joined them.

'Ohh!' Lexi gasped in awe and leaned forward in her eagerness to see them better. They instantly lifted their heads, nervously sniffing the air, then moved quickly off into the surrounding bush.

'You have to be very still and very quiet.' Morgan's unexpected voice, soft though it was, startled her, coming as it did from the shadows.

'Don't lean beyond the rail. Here. Use these.' He handed her a pair of binoculars.

'I thought you were supposed to be in the pool with Christine,' she said.

'I had more important things to do.'

She took the binoculars, aware that her hands were shaking.

She held them up to her eyes and peered through them inexpertly. Everything was blurred and out of focus.

Morgan chuckled and she felt him move in close, his breath disturbing her hair, his arms coming around her from behind to show her how to adjust the glasses to suit her vision.

'I've never used these things before!'

She was painfully aware of his close proximity and trying desperately not to show it.

'They take a bit of getting used to,' he said.

'There! How's that?'

'What?' she said, her mind having suddenly and stupidly become paralysed at the touch of his fingers on hers. 'Oh . . . yes . . . Yes, thank you. That's much better. I . . . I just move this wheel here, do I . . . ?'

Lexi concentrated hard on the scene before her, glad that Morgan could not read her mind at that moment.

'Has anyone told you that you have perfect ears?' His voice was soft in her ear and she gripped the binoculars more tightly to stop herself from dropping them. 'They're like little pink shells. As a matter of fact, right now they are very pink. Is that the sun or are you blushing?'

'Don't be ridiculous!' she said, not taking her eyes from the water hole. 'Why should I blush because the great

175

Morgan Tyler has paid me a compliment? Paying compliments to women comes as second nature to most men, after all.'

'Is that a general observation or is it aimed at me personally?'

'Does it matter?'

'It could matter a great deal, Lexi.' He took the binoculars from her and turned her to face him. 'What does it take to penetrate that iron façade you've managed to build around yourself?'

Lexi felt her cheeks redden. She twisted away from him, angry at herself for allowing him to get under her skin.

'*My* iron façade!' she exclaimed, as she moved away. 'That's a laugh, coming from you.' And she walked away and didn't dare look back.

# Christine Makes A Move

Lexi hung on desperately as the jeep bounced along through the African bush. The road they were on was a dusty, deeply rutted track. They had been travelling along it for nearly an hour.

They travelled in tandem, with Morgan and Lexi in front and William and Christine behind, separated by a huge cloud of red dust.

'Are you all right?' Morgan shouted above the roar of the engine and the crunch of tyres on the rough road.

'Fine!' Lexi shouted back and coughed as a fresh cloud of dust blew over them. She didn't envy the two in the second jeep, even if one of them was Christine. 'Is it all like this?' she gasped.

'No. This is one of the better roads!'

Morgan jammed on the brake without warning and Lexi's safety belt almost cut her in half.

'What on earth . . . ?'

'Look! On the road ahead! There! See her?'

Lexi blinked the dust from her eyes and squinted through the sun's glare. Something moved slowly ahead of them, then turned and looked at them, a doleful expression on its dog-like face.

She gasped as she recognised the animal. 'A hyena!'

'That's right. A spotted hyena, actually. Female. She's probably got some cubs nearby. They make their homes in holes in the ground and underground pipes. Look. Over there. A whole pack of them. Pass me the glasses, would you?'

Morgan focused on the group of animals in the bush. 'Ah! I thought so. You're in luck, Lexi.' He passed the glasses back to her, then re-started the engine and turned off the road. 'Let's take a closer look.'

A group of eight fully grown hyenas were resting under a tree. The animals ignored the jeep and continued with their siesta.

'Goodness!' Lexi said, 'how incredible! I never thought I'd ever see anything like this!'

Morgan smiled at her. It was a sincere smile that warmed his eyes and transformed his whole face. 'You really are enjoying this, aren't you?' His smile broadened.

'Of course I am, Morgan! Not many people get to see wild animals as close as this. I consider myself to be very fortunate.'

Morgan's hand was lightly resting on her forearm. 'I'm beginning to change my mind about you. There's obviously more to you than meets the eye, which makes it all the more difficult to understand why you got yourself involved with my brother.'

Lexi looked away. 'Haven't you ever done something rash and immediately regretted it, only to find it was too late to alter the course of things? We're none of us above the odd foolish act,

Morgan. Not even you.'

'You're right, of course!' he said with surprising honesty and sat back in his seat with a deep sigh. 'And I was a heck of a sight rasher than you once. I married my foolish mistake and I lived to regret it.'

'Is that why you're so hard on Rusty?'

'I guess I am acting like an over-protective parent, aren't I? Perhaps it's best to let people learn from their own mistakes, after all.'

'Perhaps. You can't live his life for him, Morgan, no matter how hard you try. And Rusty will resent you for it, anyway. Is it worth alienating your brother, just to make sure he doesn't commit the same mistake as you did? And so what if he does make a mistake and has to pay for it? At least he can't blame you. But he can blame you if you prevent him from doing what he feels driven to do.'

A short blast on William's horn made them both sit up and look around. The second Jeep with Christine on board had not left the road, and they could see

Christine waving impatiently to them.

'I suppose we'd better move on,' Morgan said. 'Thanks for the pep talk. You've given me something to think about.' He re-started the engine and turned the jeep back in the direction of the road. 'Let's not keep her ladyship waiting any longer.'

'Christine doesn't look too happy, does she?' Lexi remarked, on seeing the other girl's unsmiling face and angry, flashing eyes.

Morgan gave a chuckle. 'She hates safaris.'

'Then why on earth did she come?'

'Now who's being naive?'

Lexi fell silent, angry with herself for asking such an obvious question.

★ ★ ★

She tried to push the thought of Morgan and Christine to the back of her mind as the afternoon progressed. Surprisingly, she didn't find it too difficult in such a breathtaking setting as the magic of the place began to unfold before her rapt gaze. The bush was teeming with life — great herds of wildebeest with their shaggy heads bobbing; black and white striped zebra, the white under parts stained pink where they had rolled in the red earth; ostriches bouncing along on long, strong legs, the great plumes of the males undulating with the motion; gentle giraffes with huge, long-lashed eyes stretching their long necks up to the trees; massive grey elephants with flapping ears and swaying trunks keeping their playful youngsters under control.

As the late afternoon sun began to dapple the ground and turn the backs of grazing impala into living gold, Morgan turned the jeep and headed back to Keekorok.

★　★　★

'Well?' he said, giving Lexi his hand as she stepped from the jeep. 'How have you survived your first safari? Did it live up to your expectations?'

She nodded, feeling like a child in wonderland. 'It was wonderful! I didn't want it to end.'

'So you're glad I brought you?'

'Oh, yes!'

'I'm glad I did too. It was good to see you enjoy yourself.'

'Morgan . . . I . . . ' Lexi stuttered, embarrassed by the fact that he was still holding her hand. 'Thank you . . . '

She pulled her hand away quickly as Christine approached, a thunderous expression giving advance warning of her mood.

'I suppose you think that was some kind of joke,' she said. 'Don't you *ever* put me in a jeep with that driver again! Not only did he openly insult me, but he purposefully hit every stone, rut and pothole of this wretched country. Not to mention that we had to eat your dust for hours on end just so you could show your brother's ex-girlfriend a few stupid animals!'

'Christine, I'm sorry you didn't enjoy it.' Morgan fixed her with one of his cold stares which seemed to anger her even more. 'It was your decision, however, to come with us.'

Christine beat frantically at her dust-laden clothes. 'How dare you humiliate me like this!'

'Oh, you don't need me to do that, Christine,' Morgan said casually. 'You do that very well all on your own.'

The girl stared at him in disbelief before her hand came up and slapped him sharply. The sound rang out through the silent evening air.

Morgan didn't flinch. He simply threw back his head and laughed at her, whereupon she turned smartly on her heel and hurried away, mindless of anyone or anything who had the misfortune to get in her way.

'Oh, dear!' Lexi said. 'That was a bit over the top, wasn't it?'

'Christine, do you mean . . . or me?'

'Both of you, but it's none of my business.'

'Correct!'

'So I'll keep my nose out of your affairs and go to my cabin to shower and change for dinner.'

Morgan hesitated, then, his hands resting on her shoulders, he bent and lightly kissed the top of her head.

'What are you doing?' she said, but without rancour.

'I couldn't resist it,' he smiled down at her. 'Your hair's all tousled and there's a smut of dirt on the tip of your nose. Your skin's glistening in the setting sun and you're covered in dust. You look just the way you should look . . . exhilarated, full of vitality . . .'

'Oh, please,' Lexi said, although she could feel her pulse quicken and her heart miss a beat. 'I'm not so easily won over, you know, despite what you seem to think.'

He took hold of her shoulders and gave her a shake. 'I can't stop thinking about you. Is that so difficult to accept?'

Lexi gulped. 'Only a short time ago you couldn't wait to get rid of me. What kind of game are you trying to play with me, Morgan?'

'It's no game, believe me.'

'I suggest, if all you want is a brief affair, you should go elsewhere!' Lexi struggled feebly in his grasp. 'I'm not the kind of woman you seem to take me for.'

Suddenly, he freed her and she saw what looked like hurt in his grey eyes.

'You're perfectly right, of course.' He ran long fingers through his dark auburn hair. 'I'm sorry,' he said, and turned and strode away from her.

'So am I,' Lexi whispered as she watched him disappear from sight.

'Oh, so am I!'

⋆   ⋆   ⋆

The dining room was bustling with people when Lexi entered. She was relieved to see that everyone was dressed casually, despite the grandeur of the huge buffet that dominated the centre of the room.

186

The unaccustomed heat and, perhaps, more probably, the events of the day, had robbed her of her appetite. She helped herself to a glass of fresh orange and sat down at a window table.

After the first few welcome sips of cool, refreshing juice, she peered through the window at the lamp-lit terrace where couples were dining by candlelight. The scene was romantic and she ached to be a part of it. At the same time, she told herself she was a fool to harbour even vaguely hopeful thoughts in that direction. Time was her enemy. Time and her own tongue, ever ready to jump suspiciously on every word Morgan Tyler uttered.

In the short time they had known one another, she had spurned his advances more than once. Now, her departure from Kenya was an imminent reality. There wasn't time to change her tack. And he would hardly admire her for doing so, anyway. It would just confirm his opinion of her as a calculating gold-digger who was going after him now that her bid for his brother had failed.

She caught sight of him standing some way off with William. William was shaking his head, and Morgan was doing all the talking. He slapped the big Kenyan on the shoulder. William looked dubious for a moment, then laughed. They shook hands and parted, Morgan walking swiftly towards the dining room.

He saw Lexi and came over to her, nodding at the glass of fruit juice in her hand. 'Is that all you're having?' he said, with a touch of concern.

'I'm not hungry,' she replied and looked down into the orange liquid rather than meet his gaze.

'You'll be ill if you don't eat something,' he said, taking her arm. 'Come on. It's cooler on the terrace. You go and find us a table. I'll fetch our dinner.'

'There's really no need for you . . .' she began, but he gave her a little push in the direction of the terrace.

'Do as you're told,' he insisted, but with a kindly smile.

As she sat down at a table on the terrace, a young waiter rushed over to light their candle.

Morgan appeared carrying two plates of chicken salad, a bottle of wine and two glasses.

'Now,' he said, pouring the wine and handing her a glass. 'This is by way of an apology. It was a very enjoyable day, spoiled for you by my thoughtless actions. Lexi, I've never found it easy to admit when I'm wrong, but . . . well, I was out of order earlier . . . and not just today, either. I misjudged you, then followed it up by behaving badly, which has undoubtedly made you think badly of me. I hope you'll accept my apologies.'

'That's quite a speech,' her smile quivered, but came readily enough, relieved that her spurning of him had not turned him against her totally.

'I'm forgiven?'

'I . . . suppose so . . . '

'You don't sound too certain, but at least you're not throwing that glass of wine in my face and making a grand exit.'

'That's not my style, Morgan.'

'No, I'm finally getting the message on that score.' He raised his glass. 'I'd like to drink a toast.'

'All right. What shall we drink to?'

He looked deep into her eyes and she felt herself colouring.

'To the future,' he smiled, and reached out to cover her hand with his own.

'The future,' she said and clinked her glass against his. Suddenly, she felt ravenously hungry.

*　*　*

'Well, well, well! Isn't this cosy!' Christine's voice rang out across the terrace.

'Have you eaten, Christine?' Lexi enquired politely.

'I had dinner in my cabin.'

190

Christine gave Lexi a cursory glance.
'Let's have coffee in the lounge, shall we?' Morgan stood up, his hand beneath Lexi's elbow.

★   ★   ★

During coffee, conversation was hardly necessary, since the residents were treated to a noisy display of Maasai warrior dancing.

Morgan ordered cognacs all round. He handed Lexi her drink with a mischievous grimace. 'Knock that back quickly, Lexi. It'll help you appreciate the entertainment.'

She laughed. 'I am enjoying it!'

'You must be crazy!' Christine drank her cognac and indicated to a passing waiter that she wanted a refill. When it came, she stood up and put a hand on Morgan's shoulder. 'I'm off. See you later, Morgan, darling.'

Morgan looked up and frowned, saying nothing.

'Are you really enjoying this?' he

asked Lexi five minutes later, as the noise of the chanting warriors rose to a crescendo.

'As a cultural experience, yes. As a musical experience, I must admit, it leaves a lot to be desired.'

'Ready to call it a day?'

'I suppose so,' she nodded, loth to say goodnight and be separated from his presence.

'Would you allow me to see you to your door, ma'am?' He gave a little bow and clicked his heels together, making her laugh. 'You see, Lexi, I can be a perfect gentleman when I try . . . and this evening I'm trying very hard.'

'Yes, I have to agree.' She smiled up at him and hoped the sadness in her eyes didn't show in the darkness of the black velvet night. 'But sometimes you're very trying.'

'I'm not going to apologise any more, if that's what you're after.'

'I'm not.'

'What are you after, Lexi?'

'That's a leading question. I need

twenty-four hours' notice to answer it.'

They had been walking as they talked. Now, they fell into silence as they walked the last fifty yards to Lexi's cabin. Under any other circumstances it might have been a companionable silence, but Lexi was too aware of her own submerged feelings and the memory of Morgan's earlier words telling her he couldn't stop thinking about her. Whether he meant it or not, the words had disturbed her and had aroused a longing in her heart.

'Well,' he took her key from her and opened her door. 'I'll say goodnight, then.'

'Yes. And thank you for today. I enjoyed it so much.'

'I enjoyed it too.'

'Oh, I'm sure it was all very boring for you . . . I mean . . . you do it all the time . . . '

'No, Lexi, I never tire of the place, the animals This is what my life is about.'

'I can appreciate that.'

'And I think you could feel the same way . . . that is, if you stayed here.'

'Probably.'

There was another long silence filled by the chirruping of cicadas. They were standing very close. Lexi longed to reach out, to touch him, to draw him to her, to feel his lips on hers. This time she wouldn't fight him off. This time . . .

'Well, goodnight, Lexi.' He was stepping back, almost as if he'd suddenly remembered some pressing engagement. 'With a bit of luck we should see lion tomorrow. Sleep well.'

He raised his hand, his eyes searching her face uncertainly, then he was walking away from her.

'Goodnight, Morgan,' she whispered.

She closed her door and pressed her back against it, tears squeezing through her closed eyes.

\* \* \*

Propped up in bed, Lexi tried to read, but her eyes skimmed the page without taking in a word. By rights she should have been asleep hours ago, but sleep evaded her.

She glanced over to the small bedside table where her travelling clock monotonously ticked away the minutes. It was after three and she'd been sitting there nursing an aching heart and an angry mind ever since she'd heard Christine's voice as she knocked on the door of Morgan's cabin and was given entry.

Was that the meaning behind Christine's remark about seeing him later? Had he left her, Lexi, so abruptly because he had remembered his pre-arranged date with the younger girl?

Lexi beat her fist into the thin mattress beneath her. She was stupid to let it affect her. After all, she had no rights to Morgan Tyler. She had spurned his every advance and in twenty-four hours she would be flying out of his life forever. And it was undoubtedly Christine he would end up with.

★   ★   ★

The jangling of the alarm sent shock waves through Lexi's brain. She rolled over with a groan, not believing the time, reluctant to open her eyes to the new day. Memory flooded back and she sat up with a start. She must have fallen asleep after all, exhausted by the turmoil in her mind.

She jumped up and staggered to the shower to stand under the invigorating jets of water. Somehow, she had to appear calm, cool and collected when she faced Morgan at breakfast.

Just as she had dressed, she heard a light tapping on her door. She went to open it and the pale early morning sun streamed into the cabin, warming the atmosphere.

'Good morning, Miss Lexi.' William stood there, grinning from ear to ear.

'William! Is there a problem?'

'Yes . . . and then, no, Miss Lexi.'

'What on earth do you mean?'

'I have a message for you from Mister Morgan.'

'Oh?'

'He says, no rush this morning, please. He will meet you at ten o'clock for safari. He says please do not disturb him before then.'

'I don't understand, William. Is Morgan unwell?'

'Yes . . . and no.' William shrugged his massive shoulders and his grin became even broader. 'He has a hangover this morning, I think.'

'Oh, really?'

'Yes. Anyway, Miss Lexi, he sends his apologies, okay? Now, I say goodbye.'

'Goodbye, William? Why? Where are you going?'

Lexi had a sudden nightmare flashing through her mind where she was going to have to share a small jeep with Morgan and Christine.

'I'm taking Miss Benson back to Nairobi.'

'You're what?'

'Miss Benson . . . Christine . . . I take her back home . . . by jeep. She will hate it!' William gave a wicked laugh.

'But . . . but why, William . . . ?'

'That Christine! She thinks she owns everything and everybody. Morgan teach her last night that she will never own him. He told her straight! He said, *You leave me alone, you silly little fool. I don't want you. Can't you get that through your head?* Boy, she was so mad. She cried and she pleaded, but he wouldn't give in. *Get out of my sight!* he told her. When she go, Mister Morgan get drunk. I never seen him drunk before.'

'Poor Christine!' Lexi said.

'She don't deserve your sympathy, Miss Lexi, not after what she did to you.'

'All the same, William, I know how it feels to want someone so badly it hurts, especially when they don't want you . . . Well, not in the way you want them to . . . But thank you, William, for everything. You drive carefully, mind.'

'Oh, I watch for every bump and head straight for them!'

# An Unexpected Opportunity

There was a slight tiredness about Morgan's eyes when he met Lexi at ten o'clock, but apart from that, he seemed OK.

'You got my message, then?' He eyed her cagily, weighing up her mood.

'I received a rather strange message from William,' she told him unsmilingly, as she finished the last of her coffee and stood up, ready to go. 'I gather you were rather the worse for alcohol.'

Morgan's head was bowed but she caught the hint of a secret smile. She felt a twinge of annoyance because she was letting her disapproval show, and besides, she shouldn't care what he did.

'I needed to chill out,' he said, and passed her her bag. 'It's not something

I do often, I assure you.'

'Really?' She tried to appear disinter-ested. 'Shall we go?'

'If you're ready.' He looked at her curiously, then shrugged and led the way out to the waiting jeep.

The sun beat down with even more ferocity today. Already, the metal of the jeep was hot to the touch and the leather seat burned through Lexi's thin clothing.

Within minutes they were leaving the camp behind, clouds of orange-pink dust rising and writhing in their wake as the jeep rattled noisily over the rough track roads.

'I gather William has taken Christine back to Nairobi,' Lexi shouted over the noise, her words coming out with difficulty because of the jolting of the vehicle.

'Yes!' Morgan shouted back, but offered no explanation. He was giving all his attention to the road ahead, driving faster than he had done yesterday and, Lexi thought, somewhat recklessly.

'That was unexpected, wasn't it?' she tried again and clung on desperately as he swerved to avoid a pothole.

'Not really. Everything turned out exactly as I planned. It just took a little longer than I anticipated.'

'I don't understand.'

He threw her a quick look that she couldn't fathom, then fell silent for some minutes, except to point out a secretary bird strutting across the plain looking for all the world like some eighteenth-century accountant, quill pen and all.

When a large male cheetah strolled across the road ahead, Morgan brought the jeep to a crunching stop and handed Lexi his binoculars. As she focused on the sleek, spotted animal, she was aware of Morgan watching her closely, but she refused to let it detract her from the excitement she felt at being a part of this wild countryside.

'Oh, he's beautiful!' she exclaimed. 'Just look at him.'

The cheetah turned and gave the jeep

a disdainful look, then ambled noncha-
lantly away, scattering a small family of
wild pigs which ran for cover, long thin
tails held high like pennants.

Morgan reached over the back of the
seat and came up with a flask of coffee.
He filled two cups and passed one to
her.

'So,' he said, 'what is it you don't
understand?'

'I beg your pardon?'

'You said earlier that you didn't
understand.'

'Oh! Oh, it's nothing, really. It's none
of my business, anyway. It was just . . .
Oh, forget it.'

'You're quite right, it is none of your
business, but I'll tell you anyway, to put
you out of your misery.'

'You don't have to,' Lexi flushed;
embarrassed and irritated by his implication that she was some sort of nosey
female. 'Look, Morgan.' She stared
down into her coffee cup. 'What you do
has nothing to do with me. You don't
owe me any explanations. I'm just a

tourist and you're just my guide.'

'I think we're a little more than that, don't you?'

'I'm trying to be sensible,' she said, continuing to study the contents of her cup. 'One of us has to be.'

'I never know how I am with you Lexi! I can't make you out at all.'

'Well, after today you won't need to bother. I'm going home on the first available flight.'

'You don't have to, you know.'

'I think I do.'

'Very well, if that is your decision. Now, can we at least be civil till I put you on that plane?'

'Okay,' she said, with a heavy sinking feeling that told her that what she said and what she felt were two entirely different things.

'But just for the record,' Morgan added as he turned the ignition key and the engine spluttered back into life, 'and to satisfy your curiosity, Christine came to my cabin last night for as she thought, a romantic tryst, but I finally convinced her that she hadn't a hope where I'm concerned. I'm afraid I was rather brutal, but it was necessary. I should have dealt with the situation long ago, instead of just trying to laugh it off.'

'Poor girl!' Lexi said. 'Couldn't you have pretended that there was another woman? That would have put her off.'

Morgan gave a grimace. 'I did, but it made the situation ten times worse. I'm afraid jealousy brings out the worst side of Christine's nature.'

Lexi's heart sank as she pondered on his words and realised what he was saying. So that's what had been behind those shows of affection. He had been using her to get at Christine.

'Thanks a lot!' she said, and looked away as he gave her a quick, frowning glance.

★　★　★

For the next hour, they travelled in an uneasy silence, but Lexi found it easy to

204

be distracted from her innermost thoughts by the sheer abundance of wild animals that roamed the great plains of the Massai Mara. Every new species was a delight to her eye and her excitement and enthusiasm spilled over in regular bursts.

Under a line of trees along the River Talex a colony of baboons went about their daily business of eating, grooming, scrapping and playing, the babies tumbling about just like human infants. A majestic male waterbuck drank from a waterhole before lifting his horned head to sniff nervously at the air. Close by, tiny nervous antelopes, bearing the strange name of Dik-Dik, skipped delicately along, disappearing in and out of clumps of dry bush grasses. A bat-eared fox, with ears as big as satellite dishes, sat up and surveyed them curiously before disappearing back into his underground den.

The sky, too, was full of bird-life, from tiny, brilliantly coloured kingfishers to hornbills, bee-eaters, numerous birds of prey and gigantic Maribou storks.

Morgan knew them all and his quick eye picked up even the most camouflaged animal.

As the sun rose high in the sky, he found a large acacia tree and parked the jeep in the welcome shade of its branches, first making sure there wasn't a wily four-legged predatory inhabitant sitting above them looking for easy prey.

'Time for sustenance, I think,' he said, as he climbed into the back of the jeep and opened the cool-box.

'It'll be good to stretch my legs.' Lexi started to open the jeep door, but Morgan shouted a sharp warning.

'You don't get out of a vehicle in the middle of the bush,' he explained more gently. 'There are places where it's possible, but this isn't one of them.'

'Then why have we stopped here? Why couldn't we find a place where it is possible to get out?'

'Because if this is your last day here I

want you to see as much as possible.'
He looked up in the middle of
unwrapping a parcel of ham sandwiches, chunks of cheese and chicken.
Lexi had to admit she was incredibly
hungry and they made short work of
the food and the cool, bottled apple
juice. They talked spasmodically, the
conversation staying on safe ground
with questions and answers about the
animals and the terrain.

When they had finished eating,
Morgan yawned and stretched. 'I guess
I overdid it a bit last night, after all.' He
grimaced and rubbed the back of his
neck. 'Do you mind if I take a nap?'

'A nap? No . . . I suppose not.'

'I just need ten minutes,' he said,
adjusting his seat into the reclining
position. 'Wake me up if anything big
comes too near.'

'Don't worry, I will!'

'Just ten minutes. That's all I
need . . . ' He was asleep before he
finished speaking.

Lexi sat watching him for a few

minutes, then reluctantly dragged her eyes away from his face, which she longed to reach out and touch.

She tried to concentrate on the shimmering, panoramic splendour all around them, but it was the hottest part of the day and even the animals were settling down to a siesta in the shade. Soon, her own eyes began to close. She felt herself floating in space and time, strange, muffled animal sounds in her ears, coupled with Morgan's steady breathing less than two feet away from her.

She was dreaming she was at a party and dancing in the arms of a man. It was England and there were wild animals on the lawn and she was trying to warn people to run for cover, but the man kept pulling her back into the house and there was maniacal laughter ringing in her ears and Christine was there in every room and something was outside, something frightening, trying to get in. Instead of locking the doors, Lexi was struggling to open them as the house rocked on its foundations and began to slide down the hill into a deep, dark lake . . .

Lexi woke with a start and a half-strangled scream as the jeep was struck heavily by some outside force. She found herself flung bodily from her seat and ended up sprawled over Morgan, who awoke with a hoarse cry as the impact of her body knocked the breath out of him.

'What is it?' Lexi cried, terrified, clinging to Morgan for all she was worth.

'Whatever it is . . . ' he gasped as the vehicle received another blow, ' . . . it doesn't want us here!'

As suddenly as the bombardment began, it stopped. The jeep had been tipped over on to its side and had slithered down a sharp incline. There was a snorting noise, a rustling of the grass and then the sound of something heavy trotting away. Lexi could feel the vibration of its hooves as they hit the dry earth.

She made a weak attempt to get up, but Morgan's strong arms held her pinned down.

'No . . . don't move . . . not yet.'

'I think it's gone now,' she whispered.

'Maybe . . . just lie still.' His arms were around her. 'Are you all right?'

'I think so . . . you?' She looked up at him.

'Lexi . . . '

One hand came up and stroked her head, her cheek, and his thumb tilted her chin.

'Morgan,' she whispered, as his lips found hers. But the kiss was short-lived.

Lexi felt the vibration of large hooves charging, then stopping just short of the jeep.

Morgan pulled himself upright, grabbed his rifle and leaned out of the window. He lifted the rifle up to his chin and fired.

Lexi, weak, breathless and in a state of shock, crawled over to him, her eyes growing wide in disbelief as she saw the perpetrator of the attack.

A huge rhinoceros the size of a tank was standing beneath the acacia tree where they had eaten. It lowered its great armoured head and snorted, pawing the ground, while contemplating its next attack.

Morgan raised the rifle and fired again. The rhino's head jerked up, but it remained standing.

'You didn't hit it, did you?' Lexi said. She felt guilty about the rhino. It had more right to be here than her and Morgan, and she didn't want it harmed.

'Of course I didn't hit her!' Morgan said. 'This is her territory, not ours. I just want to make a bit of noise to persuade her to leave us alone.'

'Her?' Lexi blinked at the huge creature.

'Yes . . . look over there. That's why she took exception to us.'

Lexi followed the line of his pointing finger and saw something small and dark moving about in the shade of the acacia tree. She found the binoculars and focused on the shape.

'Oh, my goodness!' It was a young rhinoceros, a perfect miniature of its mother. 'Oh, that's so cute!'

As she watched, the mother rhino took one last look at the jeep, then shepherded her young charge away. The danger was over.

'Lexi . . . ' She heard Morgan's voice softly saying her name and turned to find him looking at her with a mixture of emotions on his face.

'What is it?'

He sighed, reached out and took her hand, holding it gently. His eyes looked deeply into hers and her heart lurched, fearing his words, knowing even before he spoke what he was about to say to her.

'Lexi . . . what happened before . . . when I kissed you . . . '

'Yes?' Her heart was pounding. She was sure he could hear it.

'I shouldn't have let it happen. It was wrong. We'd agreed to be friends . . . nothing more. In an unguarded moment of weakness I took advantage. It's strange the effect it can have on people when they're thrown into a traumatic situation together.'

'Please, Morgan . . . don't . . . '

He held up a hand to silence her, shaking his head, his eyes still holding hers. She wanted to look away before he saw the tears that were welling up, but she couldn't.

'Look, I'm not going to pretend that I don't want you, because I do.' He squeezed her hand, then released it, and she felt suddenly very lonely. 'The truth is, I'd give anything for things to be different, but you've already made it plain that you don't want a brief encounter. And that's all it would be. Wouldn't it?'

'I really think . . . Morgan . . . ' Lexi gulped, struggling to hide her emotions. 'I really think we should do something about getting this jeep back on the road.'

He nodded. The subject was closed.

★   ★   ★

The jeep trundled slowly back toward Keekorok as the afternoon sun turned the land to a rich, warm amber. There had been no problem getting away from the rhino's watchful gaze and although badly dented on one side, the jeep had suffered no irreparable damage.

They stopped once on the way back to look at a pride of lionesses and cubs relaxing and playing at a waterhole. It was difficult not to enjoy the scene, but Lexi did so with a heavy heart. Morgan, too, seemed unusually quiet. He was careful to stay a safe distance, even to the extent of making sure their hands did not touch as he passed her the binoculars or a drink from the cool box. Once, in attracting her attention to look at a nesting ostrich sitting on large white eggs, he inadvertently put his hand on her shoulder and removed it again as if he'd been stung.

'Will I see you at dinner?' he enquired, as she climbed wearily from the jeep at the end of the day's journey.

She had a brief vision of them having

dinner by candlelight, uninterrupted by Christine Benson. But it was a foolish dream and she quickly shook her head. 'I'm tired,' she said. 'I think I'll have an early night.'

'All right, if that's what you want. I'll have them send something to your cabin.'

'Please, don't bother. I couldn't eat a thing.'

'Very well. Goodnight, Lexi.'

*   *   *

On their return to Redlands, Lexi was greeted so warmly by Belle Tyler that the sinking feeling of regret became almost unbearable.

'Well, just look at you!' Belle exclaimed, her smile wide and all-embracing. 'You're all bronzed and you look great. Doesn't she, Morgan?'

'Yes, she does,' Morgan gave his stepmother a brief smile then quickly excused himself, claiming some urgent business that needed his attention.

'What's wrong with him?' Belle said

with raised eyebrows. 'You two didn't have a fight, did you?'

Lexi gave her a watery smile. 'No . . . no, nothing like that. Look, Belle, I really must get myself booked on a flight to England as soon as possible.

'I'm so grateful to you all for putting up with me for so long, but . . .'

'So you're still set on running away?'

Lexi bristled. 'I wouldn't call it running away.'

'I would.' Belle looked at her watch. 'Time to organise dinner. It's Maria's night off, but there'll only be the three of us this evening.'

'Oh?'

'Yes. Rusty has taken Bobbie down to Mombassa for a few days' holiday.'

'Really?'

'Yes. The boy has suddenly found some sense at last! He's stopped chasing distant rainbows and has found the pot of gold right under his nose. I couldn't be more delighted.'

★  ★  ★

Belle retold the story of Rusty and Bobbie later, over dinner. On hearing the news, Morgan's eyes narrowed.

'Now, Morgan! Don't look like that!' Belle admonished. 'Bobbie's not a child any more and Rusty wouldn't do anything to hurt her, despite what you think of your little brother.'

'I suppose you're right.'

'And what on earth did you do to Christine?' Belle went on. 'She came back in a dreadful state. She's swearing death and destruction to all men, according to her mother.'

Morgan smiled, leaned over and patted his stepmother's hand. 'Don't worry about it, Belle. Any more earth-shattering news you have to tell us?'

Belle laid down her knife and fork. 'Would you like the good news first or the bad news?'

'Belle, just get on with it!'

'Well, the good news is that the Americans have pulled out of the property deal. They've decided against a Disneyland in Kenya after all. Public opinion, would you believe, seemed to be very much against the idea.'

'Thank goodness!' Morgan's mood had lightened considerably at the news to the extent that he allowed his obvious pleasure to show as he looked across at Lexi, and she smiled back warmly.

'I'm glad, too,' she said, colouring slightly as his eyes lingered on her face.

★ ★ ★

'So what's the bad news?' Morgan asked Belle.

'Oh, dear, Morgan, you're not going to like it. It's Maggie. She's resigned.'

'Resigned! Why? Has she found another job or something?'

'No, nothing like that.' Belle sighed. 'Our secretary, it seems, is pregnant.'

There was a short, shocked silence. Lexi watched Morgan closely, remembering something Christine had said, wondering if there had, indeed, been any truth in the fact that Morgan and his secretary were an item.

'And there's a complication with her pregnancy. She's just not well enough to continue working. I've told her we'll help in any way we can,' Belle said.

'Yes, of course!'

'In the meantime, we're without a secretary and at our busiest time.'

'Have you tried the agencies?'

'No joy, I'm afraid.'

There was a short silence, then Belle fixed her eyes on Lexi.

'I don't suppose, Lexi, you would consider staying on and helping us out?'

'Oh . . . I . . . ' Lexi shook her head. 'Really, I can't . . . I have to go back home . . . I . . . '

She was looking at Morgan, trying to fathom his expression, but his face was a mask of indifference.

'Morgan! For goodness sake! Can you not persuade the girl to change her mind?' Belle said.

'I don't think anything I could say would change her mind.'

Somewhere inside Lexi, a small distant voice was crying, *Oh, yes, there is something you could say to change my mind, Morgan Tyler. Just take me in your arms and tell me again that you want me.*

Belle rose and touched Lexi's shoulder. 'Please think about it, my dear,' she said. 'The job is yours for the asking. Maggie isn't coming back. She told me so this afternoon.'

★ ★ ★

As the door closed behind Belle, Morgan looked up and studied Lexi closely. His mouth twitched into a half smile.

'Well, Lexi?' he said evenly, 'the decision is yours. Go home or stay here and help us out.'

'I don't know that it's such a good idea for us to be working together,' Lexi said falteringly.

'Don't worry. I don't spend much time at Redlands. The office is Belle's domain. She likes you a lot. It would please her if you stayed.'

'And you, Morgan? How would you feel about it?' Lexi asked.

'I won't be around much during the next couple of months. I have a couple of business trips planned. When I am around I'll do my best to stay out of your way, if that's what you're worried about.'

Lexi took a deep breath. Her better judgement was telling her to walk away from him and book herself on the next flight out of Nairobi. In fact, she opened her mouth with the precise intention of telling him that she was going to do just that. 'In that case, I'll stay,' she heard herself saying.

# Lexi Meets Maggie

The Redlands' tradition of family lunch on Sundays was something Lexi had come to look forward to and enjoy. It had not taken long for her to settle in, both as a secretary and as an honourary member of the family, largely thanks to Belle's motherly ministrations. Now that Christmas was approaching, the house was becoming more festive, with friends and business associates calling to exchange the compliments of the season.

True to his word, Morgan had been absent from Redlands a great deal of the time, and when he was at home he kept a low profile. Except on Sundays. On Sundays he joined the family.

On those occasions, he behaved towards Lexi with the utmost respect. When they found themselves unexpectedly alone together, however, his attitude changed and he became sullen and moody, any conversation between them fraught with hidden tensions. Rusty also kept a discreet distance from her, for which she was grateful.

On the last Sunday before Christmas, the gathering was large and jovial. As Lexi hurried from the kitchen with a fresh platter of hors-d'oeuvres, two things happened. A grim-faced Morgan walked out of his study, and the front door opened to admit the Bensons, including Christine.

Morgan gave them a cursory greeting, then turned to Lexi before she could hurry away into the milling crowd on the terrace.

'Lexi!'

'Yes?'

'I need a favour.' He kept his voice low, and Lexi could see Christine straining to hear what was being said. 'I have to go out. That was the hospital. Maggie was admitted early this morning. She . . . she's miscarried. She's in an awful state.'

'Oh no! How dreadful! Poor Maggie.'

'Look, tell Belle, will you, and give my apologies to everyone else, but don't mention the reason for my hurried exit.'

'Yes . . . yes, of course. Don't worry.'

★ ★ ★

Belle was saddened by the news. 'Oh, the poor woman!' She drifted away, her usual bright smile restored for the sake of their guests. Lexi handed around the hors d'oeuvres then went back to the kitchen. On the way, she met Christine, resplendent in bright pink.

'Well, well, well! I heard you were staying on. Don't you ever give up?'

'I have no idea what you're getting at, Christine.' Lexi tried to brush past the girl, but Christine barred the way.

'I mean Morgan! What else? But you don't really think he'd ever be interested in you, little Miss English Rose, do you, no matter how long you hang around him.'

'Christine, I have more important

things to do than chase after Morgan Tyler,' Lexi said coolly.

'Is that so?'

Lexi didn't answer. She didn't know what she really believed any more. She loved it here at Redlands, but she didn't know how much longer she could bear to be around Morgan, even though their brief encounters were few and far between.

'So,' Christine was saying smugly, 'the ex-secretary got herself pregnant! And Morgan rushed to be by her side. There's a surprise!'

'What are you insinuating?' Lexi's heart was beating uncomfortably.

'Do I really have to spell it out for you? Why else do you think he's at the hospital with her right now? Maggie would never admit it, of course, but we all know the truth about her and him!'

★ ★ ★

Later that day, when Lexi and Belle were sitting together over a drink, Lexi finally burst out with the question that had been haunting her.

'Belle, is it true about Morgan and Maggie?'

Belle looked up, shocked. 'Lexi! What a question!'

'Well, is it?'

'What makes you think that, dear? Has someone been talking out of turn? Christine, for instance?'

'You haven't answered my question, Belle.'

'That's because I can't, I'm afraid. Lexi, believe me, I wish I could put your mind at rest, but the truth is, I don't know. Morgan was, I know, very sorry for Maggie.'

'Sorry? In what way?' Lexi steeled herself for Belle's response.

'Maggie was in a bad way when she came to us ten years ago. Morgan came across her while she was living with one of our employees and his family. She was eking out a living by doing household chores and taking a shorthand and typing course in the evenings.'

'So Morgan gave her a job?'

'It was a gamble, but it worked out well. Maggie worshipped the ground Morgan walked on. She looked on him as her saviour, I think. But I never thought he was anything more than just kind and considerate towards her.'

Belle's head shot around at the sound of a footfall behind them! 'Ah! Morgan! There you are!'

Morgan came in and sat down heavily, welcoming the glass of whisky Belle placed in his hand.

'Thanks, Belle! I need this!' He laid his head back against the chair and closed his eyes. 'It's been quite a day.'

'How is Maggie?' Belle asked.

'Not good, as you can imagine. You didn't mention any of this to anyone, did you?' He directed the question at Lexi.

'Of course I didn't,' she told him indignantly.

He sighed and passed a hand over his eyes. Lexi looked at him slumped in the chair and felt her heart go out to him.

Loving him was tearing her apart.

'I've made a decision,' she said suddenly, forcing out the words and hearing them as if they were coming from someone else. 'I've decided to go back to England after all.'

'Oh, Lexi!' It was Belle who spoke while Morgan remained silent. 'You can't mean it!'

'I . . . I'm afraid I have to . . . I . . .'

'But I thought you were happy here with us! You're like one of the family. Is there anything we can do to change your mind?' Belle turned pleading eyes on her stepson. 'Morgan, can't you persuade her . . . ?'

He simply shrugged and stared into his glass.

'Excuse me . . .' Lexi rose and hurried from the room before she humiliated herself by bursting into tears.

*   *   *

She didn't go down to dinner that evening, but Belle, then Bobbie, and

228

even Rusty, knocked on her door to try to persuade her to reconsider her decision. Rusty, in particular, had been anxious to talk to her.

'Lexi, please don't go,' he said. 'Despite everything, I thought we'd managed to become quite good friends. And you're the best secretary we've ever had . . . honestly! Even Morgan sings your praises. I know he doesn't want to lose you.'

'Oh, I don't think he cares one way or another, Rusty,' Lexi said, biting back a tear.

Rusty looked around as if expecting to see an eavesdropper lurking. 'Er . . . look, Lexi . . . this isn't public knowledge, but . . . well, it might help change your mind if you know. Bobbie and I . . . well, we're sort of engaged.'

Lexi smiled at the news and gave him a hug. 'I'm so glad, but why should that make me change my mind?'

'I thought maybe you and Morgan were hanging back . . . you know, not wanting to hurt my feelings. After all, you and I were a bit of an item once.'

'Oh, I see. But what makes you think that Morgan and I . . . ' Her throat tightened.

'Well, you are in love with him, aren't you? And if I'm not very much mistaken, he's pretty smitten with you. The trouble is, the pair of you just can't seem to get it together for some reason best known to yourselves.'

'Oh, Rusty!' She could hold back the tears no longer. They spilled down her face and she gave a heart-rending sob as all the pent-up emotions burst from her. Anger, frustration, confusion and a deep, deep sadness cutting into her like a knife.

'It looks like I've hit the nail on the head! So why aren't the pair of you doing something about it?'

'It's no good, Rusty. There's too much baggage in Morgan's life. Christine . . . Maggie . . . more, probably. I'm not prepared to be just another one of his conquests.'

Rusty stared at her. 'Lexi, never

230

believe anything Christine Benson says. She hasn't any hope of hooking my brother. As for Maggie! Maggie worships Morgan, of course, but I can assure you there's never been anything between them.

'To my knowledge, Morgan hasn't looked at another woman since the break-up of his marriage. Now, are you sure you still want to leave?'

'I can't bear to stay, Rusty.' Lexi's tears had been stemmed, but the heaviness inside her refused to lift. 'You're right. I am in love with Morgan, but . . . oh, it's just too complicated. I think it would be best for both of us if I just left Kenya.'

And this time, she told herself, she wouldn't change her mind.

⋆   ⋆   ⋆

It seemed, however, that Fate was conspiring to keep Lexi at Redlands. The flight she was booked on two days before Christmas was cancelled due to a storm that threatened to continue for at least another forty-eight hours.

Morgan had, thankfully, gone away on urgent business, so she didn't have the pain of seeing him, knowing how she loved him, and longing for him to say the words that would keep her here. He had been expected back at Redlands long before her flight was due, but he didn't return and there was no message. They blamed it on the fact that most of the telegraph wires were down.

'There's devastation everywhere!' Belle switched off the crackling radio. 'At this rate, we'll be lucky if Morgan makes it back before Christmas Day. I do hope he's all right.'

Lexi looked up from the report she was typing, her face clouded with concern. 'What do you mean?'

'Well, he knew there was a storm in the offing. He said there might be difficulty flying, but this business deal he's gone to sort out was extremely important . . . Oh, there! I'm meeting

232

trouble halfway, as usual. After all, he's an excellent pilot and far too sensible to take that plane of his up in adverse conditions.'

'Oh, goodness, Belle! I didn't know he was flying himself! Isn't there any way we can find out if he's all right?'

Belle heaved a sigh of despair. 'The storm is raging, the airport is shut down and the phones aren't working. We can only sit and wait, and hope. I'm sure there's nothing to worry about. Lexi? Are you all right, dear?'

Lexi had gone as white as a sheet at the thought of Morgan trying to fly his small plane through one of the worst storms the country had ever seen.

'But what if he doesn't make it, Belle? What if . . . ?'

'Now, now, I thought the English were good at stiff upper lips!' Belle's attempt at humour fell flat and they both stared worriedly at one another.

'When was he due back?' Lexi said in a small voice.

Belle averted her eyes. 'Yesterday,'

she said flatly. 'He was determined to get back before . . . well, before you left . . . to say goodbye, I suppose.'

Lexi closed her eyes, squeezing the lids tightly, fighting back the gnawing fears that were rising inside her.

'Oh, Belle!' was all she could say.

★ ★ ★

It was late that same evening when something, some noise that reached Lexi through the roar of the storm, made her get out of bed and peer out of a rain-streaked window. A flash of jagged lightning lit up the dark sky, silhouetting the trees around Redlands. Other than that she could see nothing, hear nothing, except the moaning of the wind and the booming drum rolls of thunder.

She was about to return to bed when another sound, loud and from inside the house, froze her in her tracks. It sounded like a door crashing against a wall. She wondered if she should wake

Belle, but thought better of it. She put on her dressing gown and crept downstairs, her bare feet padding softly on the terrazzo tiles as she made her way down the long passage to the hall.

The front door was wide open, swinging on its hinges, the rain and wind sweeping in. Lexi could feel the chill of the storm as she struggled to close the door. Then another noise just outside, a car door being slammed, made her stop and step gingerly out on to the patio. As she did, she reached up, flicking on the hall lights so that they shone out from behind her, illuminating the figure now trudging wearily towards the house.

'Morgan!' Unmindful of the storm, Lexi rushed forward and stopped just short of where he stood, blinking at her wetly through the rain that deluged them both.

'Oh, Morgan . . . you're safe! I . . . we . . . were so worried about you!'

'I thought you'd be gone by the time I got back.'

'The storm . . . the planes are all grounded.'

'Then maybe you're not meant to leave.'

'Morgan . . . don't . . . '

Rain was pouring over them in torrents. Lexi could feel it trickling like mountain streams over her face and down her neck.

'Do you think I'm going to let you get away with this? Do you?' His eyes found hers and held them. 'You're determined to leave. Okay, fine! But you're not going before I show you just how much I feel about you.'

He pulled her to him, enfolding her in his arms. She gasped as his head came down and his lips found hers in a kiss that made her senses reel. The thunder rolled and crashed around them, but all she could hear was the joyous beating of her heart.

When he let her go, he gently placed a finger on her lips. 'Don't say anything,' he said. 'Just know that I never set out for this to happen, but you've done something to me that I thought was impossible after . . . ' He paused and then went on, 'There was a moment, Lexi, when I thought that you, too . . . '

He suddenly threw his hands up in the air. 'Oh, forget it! And I'm not sorry this happened, even though you are.'

'Morgan!' Lexi cried through her sobs as the door closed behind him. Not even the sound of his echoing footsteps could be heard above the storm.

★   ★   ★

It was late on Christmas Eve before the storm abated, but there was no chance of a flight out of Nairobi for at least two days, according to the news reports. Lexi phoned the airport and they agreed to put her on standby, but couldn't promise her when a seat would become available.

As she was making the call, Morgan came into the office and was busily searching for something in a filing cabinet. As she replaced the receiver, he turned to her, frowning, 'You will let us know, won't you, when you do leave?' He spoke with apparent difficulty, the atmosphere electric between them. 'I mean, you won't just rush off without a word.'

'Of course not. That would be . . . ungrateful. I wouldn't want to upset Belle.'

'Just Belle?'

'No . . . not just Belle. Rusty, Bobbie . . . everyone . . . '

'Nobody wants you to go, you know, Lexi.'

'Nobody?'

He hesitated, looking at her uncertainly, a troubled frown shadowing his face. He seemed to be about to say something, and then changed his mind.

They were standing there staring at one another when Belle put her head around the door.

'There you are, you two! Come on. It's time to exchange Christmas presents. Incidentally, Morgan, Maria tells me she found your hold-all and your briefcase just lying outside in the rain this morning. They'll be absolutely ruined. What on earth were you thinking of?'

Morgan glanced across at Lexi, whose face had coloured slightly as they were both reminded of his arrival home in the early hours.

'Lexi?' Belle said, puzzled.

'Excuse me,' Lexi said, aware of Belle's questioning eyes on her.

'I have some things to bring down.'

★ ★ ★

When she returned to the lounge, with festively wrapped parcels in her arms, the family had already gathered and Belle was handing out glasses of mulled wine while Bobbie filled dishes with nuts and candy. Seasonal music played softly in the background and everyone looked happy and relaxed.

Lexi's her heart ached to be a part of this, not just this year, but the next year and every other year after that.

'Here you are, Morgan,' Belle handed him some wine and beamed broadly, enjoying the occasion. 'Give this one to Lexi. She looks as if she needs it.'

As Lexi took the drink from Morgan, she was sharply aware of his closeness. He sat down beside her, his arm draped over the back of the settee behind her head, his hand hanging down, slim fingers almost, but not quite, touching her shoulder.

'Are you all right?' he muttered.

'Why shouldn't I be?' she said, masking her words from the rest of the company by dropping her head.

'You look a little pale.'

'Why all this sudden concern for my health?'

He didn't answer, for presents were being handed around, with Bobbie doing the honours, as she had done since she was small. She looked like an excited child now as she delved into the pile of parcels in the middle of the floor. But when she looked at Rusty and found him smiling lovingly at her, the little girl quickly became a woman in love.

'It seems my brother might be finally settling down,' Morgan remarked.

'I'm glad for both of them,' Lexi said. 'I hope they'll be very happy together.'

'What about your own happiness? Do you think you'll find that back in England?'

Lexi sighed deeply and pretended she was too busy admiring a silk kimono from Belle to answer his question.

As Morgan unwrapped what appeared to be the last gift, a leather-bound business organiser from Lexi, she realised with acute disappointment that she had not received anything from him.

'Thank you, Lexi! That's very useful!' He leaned towards her and kissed her lightly on the cheek.

'Hey, brother, you can do better than that, surely!' Rusty called from the other side of the room, before receiving a sharp nudge in the ribs from Bobbie.

'I doubt that Lexi would agree,'

Morgan stood up, fixed them all with a stony stare, and left the room without a further word.

'What an idiot!' Rusty banged down his glass and, with an apologetic look at Lexi, went hurrying after his brother. When he returned, he looked troubled, but tried to hide it with a forced jollity.

* * *

Belle pressed more drinks on them and Maria appeared with trays full of hot vol-au-vents and sausage rolls, thanking them all in turn for the gifts they had given her. Then she skipped off merrily to spend the rest of Christmas with her family and William.

When Morgan finally reappeared, he was dressed for going out and there was a parcel under his arm wrapped in silver foil with red and green ribbons.

'Morgan! Where on earth are you going?' Belle jumped up and laid a hand on his arm.

'There's something I must do,' he said and his eyes sought out Lexi.

'Will you come with me, Lexi?'

'Come with you? But where . . . ?'

'Don't waste time asking questions.' There was an edge to his voice.

'Just get your jacket and come with me . . . please. It's important.'

Lexi drew in her breath, nodded and went to get her jacket.

★   ★   ★

'I don't understand, Morgan. Where are we going?'

They were in the big black company car heading towards Nairobi.

'You'll find out when we get there.'

'I have the distinct feeling that I'm not going to like this, whatever it is.'

'That's a chance we're both going to have to take, Lexi.' He kept his eyes firmly fixed on the road ahead. 'I'm tired of holding back. This time I'm going to put all my cards on the table and risk losing everything.'

The ward sister looked a trifle stern as she came towards them down the corridor of Nairobi General Hospital, but when she recognised Morgan, she greeted him warmly.

'You've come to see Maggie Dennison?' her smile included Lexi, who stood uncertainly at Morgan's side, his hand firmly holding on to her arm as if he were afraid she might run away. 'It's very late, but I'm sure we can waive the rules in the circumstances. Maggie has been a bit low today. It's particularly difficult at this time of year, isn't it? I think she's still awake, if you'd like to go in.'

'Thank you Sister,' Morgan said, and urged Lexi forward.

Their footsteps echoed down the silent corridor. The hospital was bright with fluorescent light, spotless and smelling hygienically clean. They came to a halt outside a private room. Lexi looked curiously through the observation window and spied a youngish woman sitting in the bed, propped up with pillows. She had her head back and her eyes closed, lank mousy hair hanging to her shoulders. Her face was gaunt, grey-shadowed and lined with sorrow.

Morgan tapped lightly on the open door. The woman in the bed opened her eyes and squinted at her unexpected visitors.

'Hello, Maggie. I've brought someone to see you.'

'Oh . . . Oh, Morgan! Oh, I'm so pleased to see you . . . and . . . ?'

She shifted her position slightly, the better to see Lexi. Her smile was genuine, although her eyes remained sad and haunted. It was a plain face, made all the plainer because of recent suffering, but it was a good, kind, honest face.

'This is Lexi,' Morgan said.

'Hello, Lexi,' Maggie smiled. 'Morgan's told me all about you.'

'Really?' Lexi frowned, aware that Morgan was watching her every expression. 'I can't think why.'

245

'You're either very modest . . . or very foolish,' the woman said and shifted her gaze to Morgan for a split second before returning her attention to Lexi. 'Why are you running away?'

'Running away? I . . . I don't understand . . . I . . . ' Lexi shook her head, confused.

'I don't like the idea of you thinking bad thoughts about me and Morgan here . . . wrong thoughts, Lexi . . . ' Maggie reached out weakly and took hold of Lexi's hand. 'Morgan and I have never been an item. No matter what anybody tells you.' She lay back, exhausted. 'I wanted you to know that. For Morgan's sake.'

Lexi stroked the woman's hand and felt a feeble pressure as the thin fingers tightened about hers.

'Come on, Maggie.' Morgan settled Maggie gently back against her pillows. 'You relax now. It's late and you must be tired. Try to get some sleep and we'll be back to see you tomorrow. Oh, and this is for you.'

He thrust the package he had been carrying at Maggie and she clasped it to her, love and gratitude shining in her tired eyes.

'Thank you,' she whispered and looked from one to the other of them. 'Don't either of you throw away the chance of something wonderful. Grab it with both hands. It may never come your way again.'

As they left, Maggie was already drifting into an exhausted sleep, but there was a hint of a smile on her lips as she clutched Morgan's gift.

# The Words She Longed To Hear

Neither Lexi nor Morgan spoke on the journey back from the hospital. Lexi felt that she was floating in some kind of limbo. Her thoughts, her emotions, her whole life, seemed to be out of her control. She sat at Morgan's side like a puppet waiting for someone to pull the strings.

The lights were still on at Redlands, although it was approaching midnight. Morgan walked back into the house with Lexi, his hand lightly cupping her elbow.

They stopped briefly in the hall, listening to the low mumble of voices and Belle's laugh coming from the lounge. Lexi turned to go in, but Morgan stopped her.

'No . . . this way!'

He led her into his own private study with its smell of polished leather and wood and old books. He flicked the switch of a large desk lamp and the room filled with soft yellow light.

'Why?' She forced the word out from between quivering lips. 'Why did you take me to the hospital?'

'I had to. I wanted you to hear the truth and I knew you would never believe it if it came from me.'

'I see. You think I have so little faith in what you say?'

'You seem to have doubted me so far.'

He turned her to face him, brushing away a stray hair from her forehead. His eyes were dark and troubled.

'Perhaps we've been mistaken about one another all along,' she said shakily and her heart began to leap as he gently stroked her arms.

'We've both been fools, Lexi . . . allowing ourselves to be influenced by outside forces . . . letting the past intrude . . . '

'Yes.'

'I do have a present for you, you know.'

'Oh?'

'In fact, I have two, but I'm not sure that you'll appreciate either of them.'

He turned to his desk, opened a drawer and drew out two woodcarvings, beautifully worked to a fine satiny finish. One was a cheetah. The other was a rhino and baby.

'Oh!' Lexi gasped and reached out to touch them both, caressing them with the tips of her fingers. 'Oh, they're beautiful . . .'

'I wanted to make sure you remembered me every time you dusted them on your mantelshelf back in England.'

'Morgan . . . please don't . . . I . . .'

Her voice caught in her throat. She tried to move away, but he was there, holding her close and she could feel his heart beat in unison with her own.

'Lexi, do you really think I could let you leave me? Please tell me that you'll stay. Blast it, woman, I'm in love with you!' He drew in a deep breath and repeated softly, 'Tell me that you'll stay.'

Those words were all Lexi needed to hear.

'Oh, Morgan! Yes, of course I'll stay.'

She threw her arms around his neck. 'I love you too . . . so much . . . !'

They clung together for a long time, then he released her and stood gazing down at her, holding her face in his hands.

'Let's break the news to the others,' he said.

'The news?'

'That you're staying after all. And not just for a short time.'

Unable to speak, she simply nodded.

He led her out of the room and they made their way down the hallway, hands, minds and hearts locked firmly together.

Forever.

## THE END

We do hope that you have enjoyed reading this large print book.

Did you know that all of our titles are available for purchase?

We publish a wide range of high quality large print books including:
**Romances, Mysteries, Classics**
**General Fiction**
**Non Fiction and Westerns**

Special interest titles available in large print are:
**The Little Oxford Dictionary**
**Music Book, Song Book**
**Hymn Book, Service Book**

Also available from us courtesy of Oxford University Press:
**Young Readers' Dictionary**
**(large print edition)**
**Young Readers' Thesaurus**
**(large print edition)**

For further information or a free brochure, please contact us at:
**Ulverscroft Large Print Books Ltd.,**
**The Green, Bradgate Road, Anstey,**
**Leicester, LE7 7FU, England.**
**Tel:** (00 44) **0116 236 4325**
**Fax:** (00 44) **0116 234 0205**

## THE POWER AND THE PASSION

### Joyce Johnson

After a failed business venture and a broken engagement, artist Abbie Richards takes advantage of an opportunity to do a year's English teaching in Sicily. There, she becomes involved with the large, extended Puzzi family; it's members wealthy and powerfully placed in the community. Abbie enjoys the teaching and the social life at Maria Puzzi's language school, and falls in love with charismatic surgeon Roberto Puzzi, only to find herself dangerously entangled in the Puzzi power struggles . . .

# HOLD ME CLOSE

## Margaret Mounsdon

Resting actress Sara Armitage is thrilled to be offered a job, even if it means looking after Lyle Jackson's young daughter Jenny. Sara and Lyle have history and when Carla de Courcy, now Lyle's ex-wife and Jenny's mother, appears back on the scene, Sara is forced to face up to her past. Will Lyle break her heart for a second time or is she strong enough to withstand her love for him?

# LOVE ON ICE

## Teresa Ashby

Dr Becky Hope's estranged husband is dying in a hospice, his mistress at his bedside. Distraught and exhausted, Becky turns to her colleague Dr Jake Lachlan, who at first is unaware that she's married. When he does find out, wanting to put some space between them, he joins an Antarctic expedition as a ship's medic — unaware that Becky is the second doctor. Although they try to avoid each other, dramatic events on board bring them unavoidably together . . .

# THE GOLDEN CHALLENGE

## Sheila Holroyd

As Civil War looms in England, Belinda tries to escape by fleeing to France with a fortune in gold. But there are others who want her treasure and trying to tell friend from foe makes life both difficult and dangerous. And should she please her father by marrying a man she does not love? For she is increasingly drawn to a man who wants her to abandon everything she knows to face the challenge of life in a new world . . .

# IN SEARCH OF TOMORROW

## Joyce Johnson

Polly Fletcher's bold decision is to take young brother, Billy, to Australia for a better chance in life. She falls in love with rancher, Jack Peterson, but believing he is not free to marry decides to leave, but Billy runs away unaware he is in danger from a rapidly spreading fire. In the frantic search for Billy, Polly learns the truth about Jack — can she now look forward to a life of sunshine and love . . . ?

# WHERE THE HEART IS

## Chrissie Loveday

Lissa decides she has something to prove and takes a job as a housekeeper. However, with her privileged background, she's ill prepared for such work and all too often finds herself in danger of her true identity being discovered. Fortunately her boss, the gorgeous Dom, sees her other talents. He soon realises that it wasn't just a housekeeper he needed to make his life complete. But when has the course of true love ever run smoothly?